Nights Arose
By Andrea Roche

Chapter One
Sundown At Cliffside

*In Jamaica's Montego Bay, June 5, 1692, women played
the parts of lambs, but Arose had the soul of a tigress.*

She crouched on the ledge of a dune. The dying sun's
embers lit the sky just before the night arose. The previous
hours of her day were difficult and tiresome. She wasn't
sure if her queasy stomach came from her boiling blood or
the fact she hadn't eaten since morning. The day's close did
give her some relief from the evil Voodoo and treachery,
which followed her since that afternoon. Still her troubles
would not simply end because the day did. In the guise of
her alter ego, Evan, she could fool anyone. She had
perfected a manly swagger. But, no matter how drunk she
got in the pub, her troubles would remain. "He" would be
on the hunt for her, ready to pounce, like a feral animal on
his prey.

Arose held a polished dagger up to the sunlight, to
inspect the blade's oily sheen. A jewel-encrusted fleur-de-
lis adorned the pommel, glinted in the late evening sun. The
same symbol of French royal heraldry decorated her
family's coat of arms.

With a flick of her wrist, the perfectly balanced
blade spun from her hand, flipped once, and pierced the
sand between her feet. She retrieved the dagger and pursed
her lips. Specks of sand flew from the swirling calligraphy
of the monogram engraved on the shaft: NDM—Nessarose
Du Mouchelle. The "N" made her shake her head. She
preferred instead the name "Arose," as her father called
her, or even "Rosie" reserved for those who knew her well
enough. Her youth had consisted of tussles with those who

Nights Arose

Andrea Roche

Solstice Publishing - www.solsticepublishing.com

played on her name, giving her cruel nicknames like "Nessy" or "Pesty." She'd grown to hate it.

She traced the monogram with the tip of her finger and clucked her tongue when she saw the smudges left behind. Her breath came out as a steamy puff on the cold steel. Arose wiped off the droplets with her sleeve and checked the razor-fine edge for nicks.

With a gentle *whoosh*, she slipped the blade back into its sheath built into her thigh-high leather boot. Swollen eyes from earlier tears prickled, tempting her fingers to rub them until their yearning was happily satisfied. She would be much happier staying in her room with a cool cloth rinsed in lavender water, but the entity invading her home made it impossible.

She had to search for the man who could help her save her family and the dragon who taught her everything. Never having met the man, seeing him only in a vision, she would know him by his aura and his scent, consisting of iron, cedar and citrus fruit and she knew his name: St. James, Captain St. James.

Disguised in her father's old black breeches and oversized shirt, she played the role of a man as best she could. Her fingers raked her slicked back hair. A wayward curl escaped the tie that held her sun kissed locks; she straightened the hairs and tucked it behind her right ear. Linen wraps flattened her breasts, wrapped so tight; taking a full breath was a challenge. She tugged at them until she was more comfortable, and passed her hand over the cloth to see whether any bulge remained. The linen cut into her flesh; she could imagine the reddened imprints of the cloth on her skin. How relieved she would be when she could take a deep breath and rub her breasts until blood ran freely in them again.

She gazed out at the white capped sea. At the shoreline waves crashed into the golden beach. They tumbled into themselves with an unforgivable wrath, and withdrew, deserting white foam on the soggy sand. The ships anchored in Montego Bay's harbor bobbed up and down while the ocean heaved.

The clouds were painted in dappled orange and deep purple. They finally covered the burning sky. The sweat on the back of her neck dried quickly, and now the cool ocean breeze gave her a chill.

Her shoulders quivered. Shivers climbed her spine, and grew as goosebumps on her chest. On her arms, sun-bleached blonde hairs stood on end. She rubbed them to shake away the cold and felt for the bump of her muscle under the loose sleeve.

Still chilled, she turned her face to the covered sky, and let out a sigh, hoping a sunbeam would pierce the clouds and warm her face.

The sails of the English trade ships in the harbor sparkled with a pearlescent luster from the setting sun. If she ever dreamt of an excellent opportunity this would be it…she could go to the docks and sign onto a crew and escape to the Colonies or Mexico. Her large, dark Jamaican nanny taught her Creole, and Arose had practiced daily with the workers from the sugar mill; to learn Spanish would not be difficult. She nearly stood to run toward the dock. A lump came to her throat and she settled into the sand again. Her father, her plantation, and all the families living there depended on her for protection. And what would happen to Old Bess if she left? She just couldn't. Bess would never leave her if the tables were turned.

On the beach, amber reeds bowed to the gusts blowing in from over the ocean. The wind teased her shirt opened and closed. She grabbed at the collar and tied the cord tighter around her neck. She put her head down and turned her face from the blustering wind. The sand rose up, invading her eyes. Blinking, her long lashes caught the fine dust, making her eyes sting. Her tears mingled with the grains and dried to form a crust. The grit scratched at her when she brought a finger to the corner of her eye and wiped it from her skin.

Shouts drifted to her on the wind. She turned. Behind her, Le Mansion Du Mouchelle sat atop the hillside, and beyond it, a lush sugar plantation. Beyond the main house, white steam spewed from the chimney of a large green building, where even at this hour sweet juice was distilled from the cane that grew in the fields. But the source of the commotion came from neither of these. Closer, only two hundred yards away, there was a flurry of movement by the carriage house.

She stood and squinted. Voices flowed in and out of her consciousness. Images of red cloth and black sinew flashed in rapid succession. She'd been clairvoyant all her life, even before the Gem of the Red Spirit. It was as natural to her as breathing.

Figures poured out of the main house and their passions with them. Anger, worry, fear, ire—each crashed into her like waves breaking on a rocky shore. A bearded man, droplets of sweat falling to the sand, the slap of a whip, the scream of pain coming from dark lips covered in blood. She didn't know if these images came from the past or a possible future. But they flooded her mind unbidden. Then, as expected, emotions swept in. She clutched her chest and wept with fear when one person's emotions pulsed through her, after they passed, she heard the word "whore" in her mind, the unfamiliar sensations rushed through her. Intense disgust gave her the urge to spit on the group.

Dim lights emerged from the carriage house. Several people milled around the barn doors, shouting directions to each other in the dusky gloom. The usually docile mahogany stallion, Duke, bucked when they placed the saddle on his back. The barn hand settled him down, and trotted him around to rid him of his jittery energy. Finally, a rider mounted. Duke bucked again, attempting to rid his back of the bulky rider. Arose tried to make out the silhouette of who sat on the mount. From where she stood, she could not be sure, but it must have been a stranger. Duke hated strangers.

From the ascent, angry hoofbeats, and jangling chains came rushing toward where she stood. Her mouth went dry; her pounding heart surged adrenaline through her veins. They must have discovered her missing from her room when they came to lock her bedroom door from the outside to keep her from leaving.

Blinded by the swirling sand for the moment, Arose stood frozen next to the edge of the road while the large horse bore down on her. When her eyes finally cleared, the rider had almost reached her. The black cape flew behind him as he sped down the hill, an ominous bat in pursuit of a victim. Dry soil kicked up into the air while the wind whipped up small cyclones in his wake.

"Ambrielle!" she gasped. "He must be looking for me." She knew the Voodoo priestess's henchman-brother. She had watched him while he changed into a wild boar in the bog and toppled trees trying to root her out. Then act as an English gentleman caller in front of her father, in order to woo him into allowing him to marry into the family.

She dove behind the crest of a sand dune and peeked over its ridge. The sting of pebbles hitting her face and arms made her flinch, when the horse thundered past her on the road. Arose held her breath, not daring to make a move, her eyes shut tight, while the echoing hoofbeats melted into silence as Ambrielle disappeared into the town of Montego Bay. She did not move until she heard the voices fade, and the barn door slam shut. She looked out as the last of the group headed back into the main house. She remained frozen there for more than a minute, waiting to see if anyone else was on the hunt for her. Hearing nothing but the whistling wind, the rustle of the reeds and the rolling sea, she relaxed and moved from her hiding place.

Her legs wobbled under her as she moved toward the beach.

Arose plopped back down into the spot she occupied before, the curve of her buttocks filling in the divots in the sand. Still gulping air, she tried to calm herself. Her hands still trembling, she clasped them together. Holding her own hands to relieve her tension, she took a long breath in, and let it out slowly. Reminiscing, she could almost see a large hand pressed into hers, the hand of a boy she had known many years past. With Blaze's hand in hers, she felt sure, secure, and happy. At moments such as these, she missed the comfort of his company.

"Blaze," she whispered, "wherever have you gone to?"

The Gem of the Red Spirit beckoned to her as it warmed against her skin, warning her of danger. The gold that wound around the stone burrowed into her flesh, pinching at her, as the invisible cords of the opalescent gem's spirit entwined around her heart. Wincing, she tugged it from her linen corset.

Something inside her stirred. Flashes of fire exploded before her on a blood red background. Vivid bursts of green and blue danced along the surface. The opalescent gem filled her palm. Tossing it gently from hand to hand, she weighed it like a calibrated scale. The stone would gather a hearty price on the trade route, but no price could replace the sacred opalescent gem.

The spirit that lived within the amorphous opalescent gem made it all the more mysterious. She looked deeply into the spectral dome to see whether the apparition would show. Old Bess had promised the spirit would always be there to help her, and she swore to protect it. A symbiotic relationship at best, but she benefited the most. Although Arose always felt its presence, the spirit seldom showed itself. In fact, it only happened once, the day Bess the old gypsy woman first placed it around her neck.

Arose caught her breath as she thought of the last day she saw dear sweet Old Bess, at least in human form. Bess had spent many years teaching her how to harness the opalescent gem's power. Arose had already held strong psychic attributes. Not only did she possess the gift of the Knowing, but also even as a child had vivid visions of the future. After Bess bound Arose to the Gem of the Red Spirit, Arose's abilities, strength and speed had developed ten times over. And another skill had sprung from her, more mysterious and of greater import than the rest: the capacity to send her spirit into the astral plane.

Thinking back to the first time Bess had taken her to the deserts of India, Arose smiled. A small man told her the winds would help her spirit to flow from her. She had sat in lotus position on the crest of a sand dune her, bright yellow chunari billowing in the wind. Meditating until her chakras opened, her spirit transcended, pulling her high above as she held on by the silver cord, which bound her to the Gem of the Red Spirit and her corporeal self below her. Her spirit flew, a leaf tossed about by the gusting tempest. She threw back her head to look up at the sky above, the wind ripping through her hair. She lost connection with anything solid, secure, and familiar. Any fears she had melted away. Dizzy when she looked down at her corporeal self, still sitting on the ground below, she laughed, drunk in the elation of the moment.

As she grew, entering the Astral Plane had become easier. She could travel into the past if she wished. It would take only moments for Arose to watch herself grow from a child into a woman. Days, months, and years could pass in only a few breaths from Arose's earthbound body.

She sighed and stretched her legs, making herself more comfortable in the sand, willing herself not to think about the horse and rider and the curse the priestess had placed over her home. Why was Morel doing this? What egregious err had she committed? Watching as a disembodied spirit, she could find out what brought herself to this terrible point in her life, and why Mary Murphy turned from being the pious Reverend's wife to Morel the Voodoo priestess. Why she clamored after the Gem of the Red Spirit, and why she would want Arose dead.

Arose checked her surroundings for anyone who would spy her alone on the cliff. Sitting on the edge of the cliff, she willfully pushed her spirit out of her body and transported into her childhood years. Her ghostly form stood on the great lawn of her childhood home. The hot breath of the yesteryear wind blew on her face. Eager to see her childhood self, she strained her neck to get a better view. Finally catching sight of the child Arose, she watched to see what would happen next.

Chapter Two
Old Bess and the Gem Of The Red Spirit

March 1, 1681, age ten years old

The smallish Arose dashed under the kitchen window. Her tangled, wild ashen hair blew in the tropical wind. The green flecks in her golden eyes glinted in the sunlight. She cut the corner and vanished behind the palms lining the fence.

A lad named Simon followed far behind, like a sloth attempting to keep up with a gazelle. His cheeks were bright pink as he caught his breath after his jaunt. He turned, inhaled, and whistled as best he could through his pudgy fingers. Two other boys, Leon and Josiah, ran to him. Leon had light brown skin with freckles on his high cheekbones. Josiah's black hair looked as though a bowl had been placed on his head and cut, but the space in his front teeth allowed him to whistle louder than his friends.

"I think she came... this way!" Simon wheezed, still gasping between each word. He placed his hands on his knees and grunted, as if ready to vomit.

"Are you sure, Simon?" said Josiah. "If we don't find her by sundown we have to wear dresses to Sunday mass."

"I don't want to wear a dress, Jos-i-ah!" Leon whined.

"Neither do I, Leon, but a bet is a bet. An' you don't welsh on a bet." Josiah continued, "Anyways, if we find her she has to wear a dress to her lessons tomorrow."

Simon rubbed his chubby hands together. "Oh boy, I never saw her in a dress before. She's gonna hate it," he said, giggling through his words.

Making hoots and wild calls, they ducked behind the fronds of the palms. They ran through row upon row of the pointy branches. Josiah yelped and jumped into the air when a long frond pierced his skin.

"Ha...ha..." Simon pointed at his friend and laughed. Leon took a branch and poked Simon in the rear.

"Eyow!" Simon yelled. "Watcha had to do that for?"

Leon doubled over laughing. They reached the makeshift fence, which blocked off the area from the glade animals. They looked around and shrugged to each other.

Domenga stood at the back door and inhaled like a singer ready to belt out a tune.

"RO-SIE!" The deep soulful voice echoed through the plantation. "Nessarose Du Mouchelle! You come here now!" she bellowed.

The boys looked over to the dark woman.

Arose dropped off a tree branch above their heads. She smiled at her friends, a puckish gleam in her eye.

"Yes, Domenga! Here I am."

The large woman stood wiping her wet hands on a pristine white apron. She smiled when Arose came running to her.

"Sista' Bess has some 'ting for you, Rosie," Domenga told Arose in her thick Jamaican accent. "Go to de swamp near de jumbie tree. She be waitin' for you dere."

Arose beamed. She always received a treat when she visited Bess. Her mouth watered at the thought of the sweet tamarind balls Bess always gave her to eat.

She rushed up to the swamp and, as always, Josiah, Leon, and Simon followed close behind her. The boys raced along with her, laughing and kicking a ball back and forth between them as they closed in to the foot of the bog. Leon stopped short, yelling "Aaaggghhh!" Simon and Josiah tumbled into him as they halted at its edge.

Trees loomed in the shape of dark monsters. Moss

dripped like blood down their massive limbs. The three boys looked like owls, with their eyes rounded in fear. Arose could not wait for the adventure to begin.

She saw their fearful expressions and rolled her eyes. "I will go alone from here. Take yourselves on home now, and don't get lost," she told the boys and stepped into the foggy air.

"You sure you don't want us to wait for you here, Rosie?" Leon asked, not wanting to leave without her.

She stepped into the brackish water and called to them, "All right Leon, but if I'm not back before dusk, go home."

The boys cheered behind her while they scrambled up the Jumbie tree. They waved and shouted her name as she melted into the blackness of the swamp.

"Rosie! Look at us, Rosie! Look how high we are!"

Finally, well within the bog, their echoing voices could no longer reach her, drowned out by the sounds of the bullfrogs and screeching birds. Her shoes sank into the primordial ooze. The swamp smelled of rotting leaves in the still water making it hard to breathe. Dank shade made it oddly cool in tropical heat.

Arose sensed impressions of large animals that lived there long ago. She watched in awe as the flowers and animals transformed. Fruit bats became huge and took flight with a flap of their giant wings. Colorful iguanas grew in size until their dinosaur-like long necks allowed them to reach the leaves overhead. Beams of light hit her face as they ate fruit, leaves, and flowers off the top of the canopy.

She took long large strides and whispered, "Boom! Boom! Boom!" Each step resonated through the dense air. Coming across a group of giant mosquitoes, she pulled her mouth back and stuck out her tongue at them. She found a huge palm branch and waved the fronds, swatting one as it buzzed passed. It hummed louder, approaching her, Arose screeched and ran. The swarm of enormous insects closed in on her. Arose dashed under low branches and around thick trees, but the group only grew in size. She spotted her refuge; a multicolored wagon nestled on a slip of land between a fallen tree and a lake.

They were almost upon her when she hopped in through the curtained doorway. She waited for a moment watching them, daring them to come closer.

"Come on, come on," she whispered, her eyes glued to them as they approached, their stingers at the ready. She slammed the wood slat door just in time. The insects thumped as they hit. She peeked out to see them back away and disappear into the swamp. A smile cracked across her face.

Lit by only a single candle on a workbench, the interior of the cart glowed gold. An old woman sat with her back to the door. Arose crept up without making a sound until the silver tips of her ash-blonde curls brushed against the bottom of the chimes, which hung from the ceiling. They rang out in a harmonious medley.

"Hello chil'," the gypsy said without turning.

Arose reached over Bess's stooped shoulders and kissed her soft wrinkled cheek.

She looked at the iridescent jewel Bess had wrapped into a golden frame.

"What is that, Miss Bess?"

"It's an opalescent gem, a special stone," she whispered as she coiled the wire around the gem and affixed it to the yellow gold base. "It's called de Gem of the Red Spirit."

"What makes it so special?"

"For de right wearer, it can do wondrous 'tings." Bess filled her lungs with difficulty and continued, "It come from far away, from a place called Astral-lea where dey say it fell from de sky. Dere is a kind spirit who live inside. He can do magic 'tings. It can take a person far away, make dem as clear as a ghost, and see de future or de past."

Old Bess held the amulet in her shaky hand.

"How did you find it, Bess?"

"I did no fin' it, child. It foun' me, now it has foun' you." Bess finished her work. "It will help you be very strong and fast. Are you ready to do all dees tings, Rosie?"

Arose smiled and nodded. "I'm sorta' strong already, Bess." She lifted her slim arm up and curled it in, making a small bulge appear between her shoulder and elbow.

Bess let out a throaty laugh, and became most serious, "Most important 'ting, de spirit of de stone has to bind itself to you. But you have no-ting to fear."

"No Bess, I won't be afraid."

"Dat be my brave, Rosie."

She gave Arose a kiss on her head as she placed the stone against her skin.

"De spirit of de stone will protec' you always." Old Bess pressed the stone to the skin over her heart, warmth spread where it rested.

A red orange wisp flew out from the stone, a puff of smoke, which had no form. It floated around the small wagon, circling Old Bess and Arose, vibrant and alive. It brushed across Arose's curls. A ringlet of her hair pulled out straight. The specter leaped as it sprang back into place. It floated in front of Arose and halted for a moment. It turned to Bess and gave her a delicate nod. Bess responded with a bow of her head.

The apparition revolved around them, slow at first, but it picked up speed. It whirled around them, coming closer and closer, to the pair. The old woman held her head down and grumbled an ancient chant. She kept the amulet pressed against Arose's skin. The roar became thunderous.

Arose grimaced and held her hands over her ears to mute the sound.

"Look at me, chil' and have no fear."

She looked into Bess's translucent hazelnut color eyes. Spellbound, she became tranquil. They stood in the vortex of a tornado like an orange funnel, Arose's hair twisted above her head.

The wisp made one last pass and dove back into the opalescent gem. A bright orange light beamed out of the gem. Arose felt her heart open as the spirit of the stone entered. It bound her to the stone in an infinite twist. A transparent cord wound around her neck, becoming a delicate link chain, strong enough to hold the stone, but invisible to the naked eye.

The bright light fluttered and went out. Bess removed her hand from Arose's chest and smiled.

A noise came from outside the trailer.

"There it is, sir!" shouted a deep voice.

"Roger? Where did that come from?"

"I don't know. I must have passed through here ten times."

"You fools!" shouted another. "It's as plain as day and it's been here all along. Bring the gypsy out!"

Arose recognized the voice, the parish vicar.

A female voice shouted, "See if the Du Mouchelle girl is in there!" It was the voice of Mary Murphy, the town's self-proclaimed moral conscience and wife of the Reverend. She always seemed to be nearby Arose, watching her.

Bess motioned for Arose to crawl under the bench and covered it with a colorful cloth. Arose ducked down and tucked her knees under her body to make herself as small as she could.

Three large soldiers barreled into the small covered wagon as Old Bess stood to face them.

"Der be no one here but me," she said. A crash and a flurry of tings from the chimes told of the tussle that must be have been occurring. Arose placed her small hand over her mouth to stifle her own wail. One soldier pulled Old Bess out of the cart while the other two looked around for Arose.

"Ooof! Roger, move out of the way."

"No, you move out of the way."

"Do you see the kid anywhere?" Roger tossed aside a makeshift table.

"No, I don't, look under the bench there."

Charles knelt to look under it. A light came from the opalescent gem. She covered it with her hand, squeezed it with all her might, and held her quivering breath.

He lifted the cloth. His eyes passed over her without notice, her form hidden from sight.

"The child is not in here." He stuck his head out from between magenta curtains.

"Are you sure?" Mary Murphy snipped at the soldier.

"I said she's not, so she's not!" The large soldier exited the tent.

"We must find the girl! Sergeant, order them to keep up the search her in this area," said Mary Murphy.

"I can feel her presence," she hissed, looking around.

The grey-haired Sergeant shot her a look and ignored her demands. "I told you before, missus. I don't take orders from you."

"Drag the cart out and sink it in the bog," the soldier ordered. He shook Bess while he held her by the arm and pulled a paper from his jacket pocket.

He read out the charges against Bess.

"You, Bess—Gypsy woman, are suspected of Voodoo witchery, consorting with the devil and instruction of the art of witchcraft to the child Arose Du Mouchelle."

Arose caught her breath. "No...no...no..." she whispered.

Mary Murphy pulled off the silk covering from

Bess's neck and chest. There a seared mark was no longer hidden over the old gypsy's heart, in the exact size and shape of the Gem of the Red Spirit. Bess looked at her with the defiance of a much younger woman.

She leaned forward and whispered in Bess's ear, "The cord is severed; you have signed your own death warrant, old woman," she hissed. "Without the stone's protection, you will die."

"When dis life ends, another will begin. I look forward to dat."

Mary Murphy backed away a few steps her eyes narrowing. She turned to the Vicar, "She has already completed the transference to the child. We need to find her. She must subject to the trial by ordeal." Her eyes scanned the area.

"But she is just a child!" the vicar held the wooden cross around his neck in front of him like a shield.

"Well, if she is innocent, she will live. Won't she?" Mary spoke coolly. Her dark red hair, pulled in a tight bun, glistened, and her pale white skin glowed in the dark of the canopy. The vicar nodded his head, his eyes never leaving Mary's face. He trembled.

Still hiding in the cart, Arose jumped when something poked her in the side. She looked down and saw hinges beneath her. A latch held a small door closed right next to her. She pulled at it and the door dropped open. Sliding her small body out the door, the soft muddy soil squished under her feet. She hid behind a tree draped in Spanish moss.

The veteran sergeant led Old Bess out of the swamp. Mary Murphy and the vicar followed. The two soldiers remained to do the work of sinking the carriage.

With the party out of sight, Charles pulled a bottle out from the breast of his red jacket and gave it a shake.

Roger smiled and walked to the door of the wagon. He looked around and entered. Charles licked his lips as he watched him go into the wagon. He took a swig of the brown liquid, climbed up the steps, and closed the door behind him.

Arose backed away, her eyes glued to the cart's entrance. Laughter came from the wagon as she turned to run. She stopped at the sound of thunder. It came from the same general direction that the others had headed.

Arose froze in her tracks and turned to see a ball of blue fire ascend into the sky.

A screech echoed through the trees. Light brown wings unfolded and rose above the edge of the bog. The scales on the huge body reflected the low sun. A long spiked tail followed.

Bess's voice rang clear in Arose's head, but she did not sound like the weak frail woman she had come to know. She called to Arose, bold and strong.

"Run, Arose," Bess said. "They will come looking for you and de stone, de woman wants its power, and only you can control it. It is your birthright. You must not let her have it."

"Bess, what happened? Where are you?" Arose looked up at the huge dragon loomed, flapping its wings over the bog.

"About time for dat old body to die, I be done with it anyway chil'." The dragon smiled. "I have been waiting for you to come. Now I am reborn a blue fire dragon. My name will be Bessonth. Now go, I will fin' you chil'!"

Bessonth came close, and Arose saw Bess's kind eyes, the same hue as hazelnuts.

A shot rang out. Bessonth turned with an angry glare. She spewed blue fire toward the ground.

"Mary? Mary?" The vicar looked around, shaking. "Darling, where did you go?"

The Vicar ran behind a thin tree as a stream of fire and sparks popped around him. He screamed, covering his face. The old soldier pulled out a bag of black powder from his breast pocket and placed it between his teeth. His well-practiced fingers put a small ball into the end of his long shotgun. Steely-eyed, he stared down the approaching dragon.

He fumbled for the pouch and ripped it in two, spilling the black powder down his shirt and onto the murky soil. He ran to a large rock as a stream of blue fire hit where he stood. The gunpowder sparked and sizzled up the trail to the rocks. Fire exploded where the soldier hid.

Bessonth flew higher into the sky and disappeared into the high featherlike clouds.

Arose turned and ran for home. Picking up speed, she jumped over stumps and fallen trees. She leaped to a high branch. Readying her body, she swung around the branch to land nimbly on her feet. Her broad smile beamed. The whole time the Gem of the Red Spirit warmed against her skin. Her abilities intensified with each step.

She did not stop until she reached her house outside the swamp. She ducked through the window into the safety of her room.

At that moment, her stepmother, Lady Katherine, opened the door.

"Arose! We must pack your bag!"

"Why, Mother?" she asked. Tears streamed down Lady Katherine's cheeks.

"You will take a trip with Uncle Edmund." Her mother gulped for air.

"Mary Murphy had the Magistrate put a bounty on Bess," Lady Katherine continued without a breath. "Mrs. Murphy convinced her husband the Vicar that Bess has been teaching you the dark arts. They want you to appear before the town council. If they cannot agree, they will subject you to the trials by ordeal. If they do...," she halted not wanting to regret her words. Our business, our home, all is in jeopardy now, because of you and Bess," she sobbed.

"Mary Murphy," Arose repeated, her eyes narrowed in anger.

"Uncle Edmund's ship will depart as soon as you are onboard. He will look after you." Lady Katherine tried to keep her tone hopeful as she packed a brown leather satchel. She took Arose by the hand and led her out to a large black horse.

A young man of about sixteen stood next to it, holding a watch on a chain in his hand. He looked up from the timepiece and snapped the cover closed, placing it in his vest pocket. He shifted uneasily.

"Are we holding you up, young man?" her father, Francois, asked.

"Ship is set to sail in the next hour, the Captain doesn't appreciate tardiness," he answered.

His sharp, clear blue eyes opened wide when he caught sight of Arose and Lady Katherine. He straightened his back, and pushed his jagged light brown hair out of his eyes. Tall and lean, he had not grown into his disproportionately large feet and hands.

"Rosie?" Her father's voice cracked holding back his tears. "This is my brother's valet. His name is Blaze. He will take you to my brother's ship, the Royal Sun."

"Papa? Where will the ship take me? When can I come home?"

Lady Katherine glared at her husband.

"Your uncle will take you somewhere you will be safe. We will send for you when it's time for you to come back."

"Something terrible has happened to Bess! Father, you have to help her." Arose's small voice trembled, tears running down her cheeks. She pulled at her father's hand.

"The old gypsy woman, Bess, what happened to her?" her father asked.

"She's changed... She turned into a dragon....The Blue Fire Dragon... she called herself Bessonth," Arose told her father between gasps.

"A dragon, you say?" A nervous chirp entered his throat, glancing at the young boy. "Oh well, Bess can take care of herself if she is a dragon," her father stammered. "Such imagination." He looked around and smiled, then took a quick glance at the sky.

The young man mounted the large horse. Her father lifted her into the saddle in front of him.

Lady Katherine whispered to her husband, "It's worse than we thought, François. It has been dangerous for her to see the old woman. Now she is making up stories, if anyone should hear her, they will call her a witch like the rest of her mother's family." Anger seethed out of Lady Katherine and she gritted her teeth. "We have to wait till they find Bess. Only then can Arose come home. You know I love her like my own." Lady Katherine's voice had reached an ear piercing pitch. "If not, we will never have a moment of peace. Mary Murphy will run us out of town for sure. For goodness sake, your affair with her mother will be common knowledge."

"Enough, Katherine. She was my wife and the lady of this house before you. I promised her on her deathbed Arose would be protected. Foremost is her safety. Go tend to your daughters. Arose is my concern." He kissed his fingers and touched Arose's boot. "Take her to my brother now, Blaze. Tell him we will send word when it's safe for her to return."

Lady Katherine turned and walked back to the palatial steps. Her father slapped the back end of the horse and it took off running down the long road from Le Mansion Du Mouchelle family home.

The horse ran through the night to the docks. Blaze's shadow sped over the ground followed by the moonlight. Cradled deep into the young man's arms, the sweet scent of his body lulled the child and she drifted off to sleep.

A hot breath of the wind tore through the spirit of Arose as she watched from the Astral Plane, knowing full well this would be the last time the child Arose would see her father for another ten years.

She thought over what she had learned stepping back in time and the questions that had not been laid to rest while she was there. How the Red Spirit attached itself to her heart. What Bess had said could be done while wearing it. What she said when she had turned into the dragon?

"They will come looking for you and de stone, de woman wants its power, and only you can control it. It is your birthright. You must not let her have it."

Still not knowing what she meant, Arose remained in the Astral Plane. Hoping the next stages in her life would answer many questions.

Chapter Three
The Voyage To Marmara

Arose's astral form stood, like a specter, in the corner of the captain's quarters on the Royal Sun.

Edmund Du Mouchelle captained the privateer corsair fifteen years before, controlling the seas from the Mediterranean to the Canary Islands. He chased several Spanish galleons across the Atlantic and as chance would have it followed Black Bart all the way to Jamaica. He ended up in the right place at the right time, at least for Arose. Letters of marque and reprisal stuck out of his belt like a hanky, kept handy should anyone question his jurisdiction and be stupid enough to call him a pirate.

Her younger self shivered behind Blaze. He placed his hand on her back and firmly pushed her to the center of the room, as the timbers creaked with the roll of the waves.

Young Arose stared at her shoes, and she took a deep breath. Her hair, tangled during the horse ride, hung limply over her eyes.

Edmund Du Mouchelle, brass compass in hand, stood at a large oak slab strewn with maps. A feathered hat and musket lay close. His jawline and chiseled cheekbones resembled her father's but there was quite an unmistakable difference between the two brothers. Where her father's eyes were soft and happy with an innocent sweetness that emanated from within, Edmund on the other hand, possessed a shrewd awareness, a resourcefulness he had attained while surviving in dangerous situations. His salted mustache and goatee surrounded a wry mouth. Keen blue eyes focused on her as he raised a quizzical brow.

She straightened and brushed back her hair.

"So, this is the girl who has caused my brother such trouble." His lip curled up at one corner.

"Yes, Captain," said Blaze.

"She has a tongue, doesn't she?" he snapped.

"Yes sir. Well, I think so. She hasn't said much since we left the estate." Blaze's cheeks turned ruddy while he stumbled over his words.

"She can speak for herself, then." Edmund's voice resonated around the room, more accustomed to shouting over a melee of cannon fire than speaking to a ten-year-old girl. "I have no nursemaid here, young lady. No pretty dresses, nor anyone to curl your hair."

"I don't care about those things." She shrugged and met his iron gaze with her own version of steel.

Edmund looked up at Blaze with a wink.

"You don't play with dolls and wear pretty bows in your hair?" Edmund's eyebrows rose.

"No, I've never had any use for them. Have you?"

Edmund was taken aback, "There have been a few dolls I have enjoyed time and again, but never you mind." Quickly remembering to whom he was speaking, he laughed roundly, "I think we shall get along splendidly!" He turned to Blaze.

"Let's start with getting her a pair of britches and waistcoat. Do you have something that would fit her?"

"Yes, Captain," Blaze replied.

"And crop that hair. Those curls will give her away."

"Come with me." Blaze took her by the hand and led her from the door to the main deck. The helmsman held tightly to the spokes of the wheel. Stars were fading in the dawn sky, while the ship glided past an orange sun.

They were already at full sail and had caught a good wind. Exhilarated, Arose ran to look over the ship's rail as they sped along the crested waves. She watched the dark water below her was sliced by the wooden bow. Gulping salty air, she giggled as sea spray tickled her cheeks.

Blazed pulled her away and bustled her to the steps leading to the quarterdeck.

One of the crew, just waking from a drink-induced sleep, slogged to the rail. He unbuttoned his breeches and sent a stream overboard, emptying his full bladder. He watched over his shoulder while they made their way on deck.

He stood in front of them, blocking their way below deck.

"What do we have here?" He examined Arose closely. "That's a nice bauble you have around your neck there, Missy. Let's see it."

Blaze pulled out his dagger. "Back away, you slug, this child is the captain's niece. And you aren't gonna touch her."

The seaman sneered at Blaze. "Do you think I can't take you out, boy? Then bring her below deck and have my way, before the captain's any the wiser?"

"No! You won't," said the lean young man, tall but only half the weight of the brutish pirate. He posed bravely, waving the blunt, rusty blade at the sailor.

The thug smiled, with all of his rotten teeth showing from an unshaven and dirty face. He put his grizzled fist on Blaze's shoulder and gave him a hard shove. The rusty blade fell from his hand and bounced along the deck. Blaze stumbled backward, falling down the stairs and hitting his head, knocking him unconscious.

The sailor and Arose dashed for the prized weapon, but he made it to the blade first and pushed her away. She fell on her backside. He snatched it up from the planks. Turning to Arose, he put the point to her throat. He hissed out a long, wheezing breath. She looked down at the roughly sharpened blade.

Her heart began to pound in her chest and raw adrenalin coursed through her veins like never before.

The Gem of the Red Spirit glowed from her chest. The sailor made a quick lunge for the radiating gem. It came to life in an instant. The warm fire of the passionate spirit in the opalescent gem surrounded her in vermillion. Arose, shielded by an impenetrable sphere, lifted into the air. Her eyes beamed red as her body lifted as if pulled by a rope tied to her chest. Her hair blew up with the wind in a tempest that spun within the crystalline sphere.

"She is bewitched!" he shouted, stepping away from the glowing globe, backing up to the ship's rail.

The sailor frantically looked around, gasping as his bare feet slid on the deck. Suddenly the ship pitched, his feet flew into the air, his head down, over the ship's rail. Grabbing helplessly at the polished handrail, he fell backward overboard. A quick scream echoed out and silenced as the ship sailed on.

The bright wisp pulled away from her and seeped back into the gem on her chest. She alighted gently on the wooden deck. Everything became as silent as before. She felt the sea spray tease her hair while the wind hit her face and the rush of water drove the craft under her feet.

She ran down the stairs and crouched over Blaze, lying sprawled below deck.

"Are you all right?"

Blaze sat up like a shot and stared at her, bewildered.

"Where is that dodger?" He looked around, holding his head. "Oh, he went away," she said, pointing toward the stern of the ship.

"Where is my dagger?" He looked around the floor and back at her.

"He took it with him when he left." She helped him to his feet and he dusted off his pants, the incident with the sailor ancient history.

He looked at her and rolled his eyes. "Come on, we have to be sure you don't get pegged as a girl again. Let's find you some trousers and a shirt. You are going to need a boy's name, too. What do you want to be called?"

She cocked her head and thought for a quick second. "How about Evan? I like the name."

"Okay 'Evan', tie back those mangy curls," he said with a tug on her hair.

The two climbed up the stairs to the main deck.

"You owe me a new dagger," he said, elbowing her.

"Hopefully it will have a better edge," she said, and elbowed him back.

"What would meet your approval, Miss?" He bowed deeply. "I'll bet something that looks like a rose with plenty of thorns so it will be just like you." He playfully mussed her hair.

She looked up at Blaze and nodded with an impish grin.

***

From that day on, she and Blaze spent most of their time in top sail. They shouted at the wind as it blew through their hair.

"Hang on, Evan!" He held her hand, dangling her high over the ship's bridge. The horizon bobbing in and out of view as they swayed over the ocean.

Concentrating on the platform at the top of the mainsail, Arose swung her feet out to land on it. She let go of Blaze's hand and pulled herself up. The Gem of the Red Spirit glowed, as she reached the wooden slip, no wider than a barrel crate.

Blaze climbed up to where she sat smiling.

"You like taking chances, don't you," he said nervously. She nodded and batted her eyes.

He held onto her as they dangled their feet high above the deck.

Keeping the crew at bay, Blaze kept a close watch on Arose. He became nursemaid and best friend to her, sharing her laughter and tears.

From her vantage point on the Astral Plane, Arose realized how her power was so strong. Not only had the Red Spirit given her strength. Her power lies in the symbiotic combination of both her wild heart and the Gem of the Red Spirit. The crystal globe that surrounded her and what had happened while she was cocooned within was the key.

Chapter Four
Landing In Marmara

December 2, 1685, age fourteen years old

*Y*ears later, after many ports of call, Arose had begun to sprout, growing to be almost as tall as her best friend, Blaze. In addition, her legs were not the only things sprouting; she began hiding her blossoming breasts with strips of linen. She had begun to bleed. For a few days each month, she found herself in a mess when she woke. She felt weak and looked pale. Her uncle took note and sailed to where she would be safe from the forces in Jamaica.

They awoke early one morning as shouts of "Land ho! Ready the anchor, ye scabrous dogs," rang through the quarterdeck.

The door next to Blaze's bed slammed open, and the first mate stuck his head in.

"Cap'm is looking for ya lad, and bring the boy with ye."

Arose packed her britches into a leather satchel. Quietly she made her bed and put her boots on. She shoved her ashen tresses into a knitted cap and checked her look in a reflective pewter plate.

She placed her hand on her cheek and passed it along her lips, biting down on them to give them a rush of blood for a pink hue. She pulled out a few strands of hair from under her hat and stared at herself. She smiled coyly, emulating the sultry expressions she had seen from even the courtliest of ladies.

The door slammed wide open and Blaze stood in the doorway. "What are you doing?" he asked looking at her quizzically.

"Nothing! Nothing!" she snapped back at him. She tucked her hair back under the hat and wiped the gleaming wetness from her lips. She walked out of the room. Passing him in the doorway, their bodies came close; she felt a rush as she brushed past him. Their hands touched.

"Excuse me," she stammered, turning to look deeply into his blue eyes.

"What's wrong with you this morning?" He scowled at her. Arose dashed to the main deck, a full blush in her cheeks.

The ghostly Arose stood watching, while her younger self ran from the room. She watched as Blaze looked down at his hand. He slapped his hat on his head and followed her up to the main deck.

***

Her uncle commanded the ship be anchored at the port in the Sea of Marmara near his home, a gift from the Sultan. He decided there would be the best hiding place for her, far up through the Mediterranean Sea.

They walked out on deck as if they were heading for the gallows. The shore of Constantinople looked majestic off the port bow. Tall, oddly shaped spires sprang up over the town. Brightly colored buildings dotted the high cliffs.

When they entered the captain's quarters, Edmund stood at his window, dreading to hear the argument both would pose. His hands clasped behind his back. He turned to the young people before him. Instinctively they broke out into an incoherent cacophony. He raised his hand and they silenced.

"You cannot stay here, Arose. You are growing into a woman. It's becoming harder to hide that fact every day." He spied a look at their dejected faces.

"Come now! This is not a death sentence. Maybe

someday you both will cross paths again. Right now, you are required to tend to your lessons, Miss, and you, young Blaze, have a lot to learn before you can captain your own ship, my boy."

They sheepishly left the room and walked out to the deck. They stepped into the small boat and she settled in while Blaze pulled the ropes lowering the dinghy into the water. They paddled their way to shore.

An Englishwoman stood on the dock, waiting for them to arrive, her black hair tied back in a neat bun. Blaze landed the boat as Arose jumped out and tied it to the post.

Blaze stepped onto the wood dock. "Keep a weathered eye out, mate." He spat on his hand and held it out to her.

She stared down at his hand. A lump in her throat made it hard for her to look him in the eye, her tears welling up.

Blaze smiled hopefully. "Don't hang the jib, I will see you soon."

The woman strained to see around them, and then looked down at the boyish Arose. "Who is this?" she said in a curt voice. "Captain sent word we are picking up his niece?"

Arose pulled off her hat and let her ashen tresses fall. The woman stepped back, almost falling off the wood slat dock.

Arose couldn't hold back any longer. The thick exterior she tried to hold up for so long melted when being torn from Blaze. She leaped up at him, holding him around his neck. His arms wrapped tightly around her waist. They rocked side to side for a brief embrace. She quickly kissed him on his cheek and let go. Blaze blushed profusely, his cheeks and ears burning red. Arose turned and ran to the carriage, holding back sobs. The governess gave a sinister last look at Blaze and lifted her long skirt, and with a flourish followed Arose into the carriage. The driver clucked his tongue to the horses, the carriage moved off down the cobblestone street.

Blaze stood alone on the dock while they rode away, his eyes watching intently. She stared at him through the back window.

He pulled out a gold pocket watch and stared down at it, then snapped it closed and put it back into his pocket.

Arose and her new English governess drove through the streets of the small island. Passing carts selling the largest papayas she had ever seen. Red and gold carpets laid on the side of the road while women haggled over the price of eggs.

They reached her uncle Edmund's lavish estate near Constantinople, on the edge of the island in the Sea of Marmara. The yellow stucco home sat built into the cliffs overlooking the blue-green sea. Its only tenants were Arose, her governess, and a handmaid who doubled as a cook. It had four floors with twelve finely appointed bedrooms, and even boasted running water carried to the kitchen and water closets by terra cotta pipes.

Still, for Arose, living in the big empty house was torture. She missed her Uncle Edmund and working on board the ship. She missed her studies in language and art. Diving into the myriad of books that lined the Captain's chambers had become her selfish indulgence.

Most of all, she missed Blaze.

Charlotte Von Strad, her governess, was a difficult woman to please. She demanded perfection in Arose's posture and manners, and saw to it that she wore a corset daily.

Months passed. Arose was kept under Charlotte's watchful eye. She kept herself busy with the books Blaze gave her from his studies. She either read at the table or sat with her knees up close to her chin, in the highest level of the cavernous stairwell. She would look up and yell, "Hello!" waiting for her echo to answer her.

One day after shouting out her greeting the Governess's voice rang back.

"You are late with your deportment exercises, young lady. Did you forget to wear your corset again?" The governess stood over her with a stern look, then walked into the sitting room outside Arose's bedroom, beckoning Arose to follow. She walked to the wide table, where books were scattered everywhere. "Put away these books. We must work on your diction and etiquette. Your years at sea has left you sorely lacking in manners."

Arose gave her a sideways look.

"That's exactly what I mean! You are very rude. No telling what bad habits you picked up on board that ship, living like a man. You must learn manners!" The woman sniffed and turned her head, "You haven't the first clue about how to pour a proper cup of tea."

"Blaze didn't think I needed to learn those things. He's been teaching me mathematics and spelling. We spent hours reading together. He taught me poetry and philosophy. Blaze and I..."

The woman's face flushed with anger. "I have heard enough of that name! The nerve of that Uncle of yours, allowing his porter to teach you that heresy!" She lifted her arm and pointed to a thick wooden door. "Go to your chamber until you are ready to practice your deportment. In the meantime, I will get rid of these, so there is no more temptation."

"No, you won't." Arose grabbed several thick books and ran to the door, "You can't stop me from thinking!"

She grabbed Arose's arm knocking the books from her. The door to her room close by, the woman flung her like a ragdoll through the air and into the dimly lit room. She landed with a thud inside. The door slammed behind her, and the tumblers fell, telling her she had been locked in. She took the opalescent gem out from the collar of her blue gingham dress, which now had a tear at the knee. A small, high window facing the ocean was the only light. She pulled over a chair and stood on it, becoming as tall on her toes as she could reach. The Gem of the Red Spirit began to glow, reaching out over the sea like a beacon.

"Come on, Blaze. See this! Somebody see this!"

She stared out hoping to spot the familiar sails of her uncle's ship. Sharp rocks and churning waves lay below.

She cocked her head when she caught sight of a large bird heading directly for the island. A long neck and scaly head came into view. Sharp fangs glinted in the sunlight. It followed the red glow of the opalescent gem.

The handmaiden carried in a tray of tea. "That's a dragon," Arose said, pointing.

The handmaiden peeked through the window. The tray flew into the air as she ran screaming from the room. Arose did not move, watching unfazed as the large dragon closed in.

Its nose stopped just inches from Arose's window. Arose examined the dragon. Its eyes were the color of hazelnuts. Arose broke into a wide smile.

"Now where be dat nanny?" Bessonth's teeth gleamed.

Chapter Five
The Birth Of The Demon Slayer

September 26, 1687, age sixteen years old

The elder Arose watched eagerly while the years ensued for her teenaged self. Looking for clues to win battles not yet fought. Day after day, she watched as Bessonth the dragon came to the balcony in Marmara. Sometimes still asleep in her mosquito-netted bed, Arose woke to Bessonth's hot breath. They would disappear for hours and sometimes days. She spent her time learning the craft of the opalescent gem

Under the olive branches in Egypt, she sent her gossamer essence out into the blue, holding onto her body by a silver thread. Able to go anywhere, she knew where her heading would be.

She found Blaze, now just a few years into his twenties. She lingered above him as he climbed the ratline rope up to the pigeon's nest of a large ship. His light brown hair played over his sparkling eyes. His face and finely chiseled chin beamed in healthy handsomeness. He pulled an axe from his belt, muscles in his forearms bulged as he cut the ties of the main sail. It snapped to its job and quickly billowed. She watched his eyes after a job well done. Full of joy, he smiled and laughed into the wind.

Arose felt an unfamiliar pang. She missed him so much, but his years aboard the ship had made him forget her. She stayed and watched while he made his way down to the main deck. Ship hands patted his back and called their congratulations out to him. He looked up to the sails

and smiled while she floated within, peeking out from behind the silks.

Right then she despised her life. She wished she could join him in the revelry on deck. She tugged on the silver cord and it splintered in her hand. Arose felt a pull on her arm. She turned to look, and next to her were two black swollen eyes. A pale face appeared, round, with peaked brows.

"Who are you? Let me go!" she cried to the spirit next to her.

"Let me have it! Give me the Gem of the Red Spirit!" he growled with a fearful trill in his voice. He tore at her arm and pulled her farther out into the spirit realm. A pathway stood before them; black wrought iron gates blocked the way. She yanked her arm away from him. His nails sliced into her.

"You don't want it, give it to me!" he screamed, wildly.

"No! Leave me!" Arose pushed him, seething.

He backed away immediately. "All right then, we can make a deal." He spoke quickly, wringing his clawed hands, his long tongue licking his lips.

"The Red Gem around your neck is the key to the Netherworld. You have the power to free the spirits imprisoned there. If you open the gates, you will be Queen to the demons—for centuries. Riches, jewels, power. Even the handsome young man on the ship can be yours!"

"Blaze!" she gasped, giving away what her heart already felt.

The demon trembled with excitement, "Yes! You want Blaze? I can make that happen. He can be yours, he would worship you, beg for your love. All we ask is that we enter the mortal world, be free among the good people there." He laughed nervously.

Her almond eyes narrowed, "No, I don't want any of that! I don't want to be your queen," Arose pulled away.

"I will never let you enter the mortal world."

Suddenly, a huge black arm came out from between the bars and swiped at her. A growl followed. Instinct caught Arose in its warm breadth. She held out her hand, and concentrated intently, A golden sword appeared in her fist, a thick heavy broadsword, glowing iridescently.

She did not want to show the round-faced creature her fear and give him the advantage, but she had already played that hand. Now she had to surprise him with her courage.

The creature pulled out a thin curved blade and made a figure eight in the air. Arose shot him a look as the corner of her lip turned up. She caught the fear in the demon's eyes, making her a bit more confident. He charged her with a shriek, swinging the blade before him. Arose met his sword with an upswing, the golden sword sung as it cut through the cloud-filled air, a clang sounded with the clarity of a bell. The heavy blade sent the creature back more than a few steps. Arose prepared herself for another onslaught. The creature sneered at her, making Arose grit her teeth in anger. She spun herself, hurtling through the air to meet the flesh of her opponent's midsection. The creature dropped to his knees while a chorus of screams sounded from behind the thick gates of the Netherworld. She looked down at the creature and watched the black blood spill out of its neck. She could have left him at that, showing mercy for what would be her first kill. The howls from behind the gates turned to complete silence, all watching in what would be the most telling, for either she would be undeniably the declared the Demon Slayer or she would be deemed weak and the challenges would continue until she herself would be overrun.

She looked at the creature and knew what she had to do; the fate of the mortal world would be in her hands. She raised her sword and smiled before she struck. Ending any doubt that she would be sentry defending the mortal world

from the creatures imprisoned in the Astral Plane.

Finally, she turned to see a bright light. "Bessonth!"

Arose fell to her knees before Bessonth, exhausted from her trial.

"You must keep your mind free of fear and doubt. You must not let it consume you." Bessonth begged of her.

"The creature made empty promises, he brought you to the gates of the Netherworld and promised all sorts of t'ings, but you have to be beyond temptations. No matter what he say, you must never be open the gates, chil'. Once opened, the evil there can consume the earth." Bessonth smiled in her dragon way, knowing that her decision to give her the Gem of the Red Spirit was the right one.

"You must be strong and look to the good. Keep the evil inside the gates, and never, never open them."

"He told me I can be with Blaze again. He promised Blaze would love only me if I let them go."

"They can't make Blaze love you. If he wants to be with you, he can be. Only he can make that decision, not that creature. Also, be careful you do not fray the silver cord, if it breaks and you are caught between worlds, any wandering spirit can enter and claim your spiritless body. They can claim the Gem of the Red Spirit and the key to the gates of the Netherworld."

The thought chilled her.

Finally, a day came when Bessonth did not return. Arose frantically watched the horizon for her dear dragon.

Soon after, a letter came from her family for her to return home. She tearfully left the balcony only when her Uncle Edmund personally came to bring her to the ship. She left word with the chambermaid, if Bessonth did come looking for her, she had returned to Jamaica and could be found there.

***

April 20, 1689, age eighteen years old

A somber Arose arrived at the port of Montego Bay aboard The Royal Sun II. She had seen neither Bessonth nor Blaze during the trip from Marmara. From where she stood on deck, the town looked small compared to the lavishness of Constantinople. People stopped to stare as Arose stepped down the gangplank. People whispered the words, "heiress" and "Mansion Du Mouchelle." She turned to smile, but they just bowed or turned away.

She landed once again in the port of Montego Bay, more of a woman than most of the town's females of the same age. Her wide brimmed white hat shaded the sun from her eyes. Blonde-streaked hair gently tumbled over her shoulders.

The carriage rumbled down the dirt road toward her home, bringing her back to where the chase ended, more than ten years from the day Bess gave her the Gem of the Red Spirit. She passed row upon row of sugar cane. Workers carrying bales of cut stalks edged the road.

The time she spent away from Jamaica had worn hard on her father. He stood on a platform in the hot sun, watching the field workers lift circular stacks of cane into the mule-drawn cart and marking a record on the board in his hand.

"Stop the cart, please." Arose stepped onto the dirt road and walked to her father. She placed her hand gently on his shoulder.

He looked up at her, his puffy eyes and tanned skin crinkling with a smile when he caught sight of her. He looked as if he had been ill and working too hard.

"Father," Tears and pity were in her eyes seeing her father so exhausted. She placed her hand on his cheek.

"I have no sons," he said sadly.

"I am here now, Father, I will help." She called to a tall thin worker struggling with a heavy bale of cane. He looked, young, smart and honest. "What's your name?" she asked with a smile.

"Ephraim, Miss," he answered shyly.

"Great name." Her smile glowed. "It means 'fruitful'."

His tense shoulders relaxed, and he broke out into a trusting grin.

She looked at him thoughtfully. "If I give you this job, can I trust you to do the right thing?"

Surprised, the young man nodded. "Yes, Miss."

The man came and took her father's place on the platform. She took the board from her father and gave it to him. "You keep count. We will be back."

She and her father walked through the sugar stalks. He pulled a stalk and handed it to her. Arose was struck by the beauty of the thick green branch. Something stirred within her as pride swelled in her chest.

"This is your land, Rosie; someday this all will be yours."

Arose nodded and tried to summon a smile. "Father, time for you to rest, I am here now."

He walked slowly to the door.

From then on, she took the duties of running the plantation from her father. Ephraim took the job of her second. She gave him title to his own home in return for his duties. At dinner one night, she announced to her parents, "I am giving amnesty to all who are living on the grounds."

"It's your business. Do as you please," her father said, and turned his attention back to the slab of spiced beef before him.

The workers traded their daily toil in the field for food, clothing and shelter the Du Mouchelle Plantation provided. Arose made sure their families had all they required and were cared for. Schools were in place, medicines were available, and music lessons for anyone who wanted even though more than one time she would be the student. The children loved to sing and dance, taking her by the hand to teach her the steps to dances, which seemed too complex for their tender age. Quaint cottages replaced shacks; flower baskets hung from the ceilings of brightly colored patios. Happy children played and learned in the sun.

So consumed with running the plantation and mill, she had time for little else. Her gentle yet commanding ways made her more familiar with the workers than with her sisters, who made it a point to never step foot in the sugar mill.

She wore the Gem of the Red Spirit around her neck but barely used her abilities. She put her Evan persona away for a time. She only donned her black breeches and shirt when she got a hankering for a pint in town dressed as Evan to Montego Bay or even the Port of San Sabastian on the other side of the island. She once again found her childhood friends Josiah, Leon and Simon. Still cohorts, they unwittingly welcomed her as Evan into their circle.

In her womanhood, her easy smile and a flirtatious manner made her the focus of chatter around town. She enjoyed a stroll every now and again, dressed in an attention-grabbing ruffled frock, her hair piled high on her head in the latest fashion.

***

June 5, 1692, Present day 10:00 AM

The day before, she had told Ephram of her plans to go into town. She had prearranged to take a day away from the rigors of the plantation. Maybe spend some time at the bookstore and silently read. Instead of a book, she would delve into people's thoughts or perhaps take a soul walk through someone's life. She giggled at the thought.

Duke, her favorite horse, stood complacent and ready to go into town for a day's adventure. Arose's spirit watched her embodiment pass her on the road while her breasts bobbed along to the rhythm of the horse's trot. A sun-streaked curl caressed them at their fullest. Around her neck, the delicate yet strong chain dropped the Gem of the Red Spirit neatly between her breasts over her heart. She rode into the town.

She tied the dark brown stallion to the post near the apothecary and walked toward the gathering by the town square. She clicked the heels of her white lace-up boots as she hurried across the cobblestones. Blue ruffles and white lace flashed as she lifted her long skirt to avoid the mud puddles in the street. A cloudless Caribbean sun beat down on the crowd.

Mystical forces threw open her mind's eye as she scanned the passing faces. She usually could tune out voices, but today they burst through every blockade she put up. Impressions flooded in, like the wind of a hurricane through a door, which refused to close. A jumble of voices resonated in her head; she tried to make sense of them. She focused her thoughts.

"One...at...a...time!" she said squeezing her eyes closed tight, straining against the flood.

She concentrated on a large bellied man closest to her,

I hope the cook made an extra mince pie just for me.

A giggle echoed, as a young girl stared into a dress shop window,

I wonder how low I can my get my neckline before mother has a canary.

A wealthy housewife passed by,

Look at me! Look at me! I have three servants behind me, all with large packages from the store. She looked around and saw Arose staring at her. She flashed a haughty smile.

Do I know her? No, I do not. I hope I see someone I know...Look...at...me! She commanded.

The voices trailed off in her mind. She laughed to

herself about the how frivolous their lives were. Going through life not realizing how precious their lives were and how close to the Netherworld they were. She walked with a purpose, every fiber of her being sharp and aware.

She headed for the bookstore at the end of the courtyard. Her quick gait highlighted the bounce in her breasts and the roll in her hips. She stopped at a window and pulled a few strands of hair out from under her bonnet. The new look softened the sharpness of her high cheekbones. She bit her lips and smiled when she saw a pinkish hue come up.

Crowds of onlookers lined the street as the parade of red-coated young men passed on their way to the docks. Tall ships occupied the harbor; their hulls creaked as they strained against the mooring. Their heading would be England or the Colonies.

Arose stood out from the crowd, being a head taller than most of the ladies waving their lace handkerchiefs. She stopped briefly to join the giggling women gathered before the barricades.

The soldiers' feet hit the cobblestones in unison to the drumbeats, in perfect step. She could take out her lace hanky and wave, or she could cheer them on to their ships, but she had pity on them and said a quick prayer for them instead.

She had seen what they were up against firsthand and knew what would befall them even before they reached their destination. Most would suffer from an onboard disease or die in a pirate attack. Her eyes welled up for a moment, as the last of the troops turned the corner.

"Hoy! Hey, you keep going," shouted the smallest of three street tramps leaning against the slats of the general store. He ran down the center of the street and kicked his foot in the air in a mock swift kick behind their backs.

"Ha…Ha…Liam. I think you can take them down," said a bald headed gravelly looking man, as he pushed tobacco into a cornhusk pipe.

The young man swaggered his way back to the group, proud of himself for his bravado. "These blokes come passing through our streets thinking our ladies will swoon at the sight of 'em."

"Have some respect for those brave men. They have much more courage than you."

The words flew out of her mouth before she had the chance to stop, breathe and think.

The townsfolk began to clear the street, looking fearfully from the young men to Arose. A short housemaid in a worn woolen dress ran up to Arose and grabbed her by the arm, pulling her down to speak in her ear. "Do you know who those boys are?" she said in a gossipy whisper. Arose shook her head, no.

"They are trouble, let me tell you!" she continued in a low husky voice. "Brothers." She nodded as she spoke. "Shaw, Faolan and Liam. Hellraisers, the lot of 'em. You be best to be on your way, Miss. They have sullied more than one woman's good name."

"Thank you, I will keep it in mind." Arose pulled away from her and turned to face the brood.

The woman scurried back to the plank boards of the storefront. "She's on 'er own now. It will be on 'er own head what happens!" she grumbled as she wobbled in through the paned glass door.

Now the street was empty except for Arose and the three brothers.

"Not such pretty words from such a pretty face." Faolan, the middle brother, circled her as a vulture rounds a carcass. Cold blue eyes stared out between strands of greasy, jet-black hair covering his forehead. The sun had burned his unprotected face. Red blotches covered his raw skin. He pulled at suspenders holding the waistband of his overly large pants up to his chest.

"Aye, a lass as lovely as her you don't see often,"

said Liam, peeking out from under his tweed cap. The youngest, Liam, shy of twenty by about two years, taller than either his brothers were. His curly, dark blond hair framed a pleasant face. He smiled flirtatiously at her.

"I haven't seen this one around here. She must be new," said Shaw, approaching her from behind. Faolan fell to one knee before her.

"Marry me, Miss. I will make an honest woman of ye... before I bed ye." He turned toward his brothers with a smile. The others stepped closer, surrounding her and closing in.

The amulet warmed to warn her of danger. A chill ran down her spine. She knew if she showed fear, they would sense it and the next day she'd be found behind the shed of the apothecary. She gave a lift to her brow and severed Faolan with a look. He backed away and skulked behind the building.

Arose saw her opportunity to walk away. She took a quick step, but Shaw stopped her cold. He grabbed her elbow and squeezed it, akin to a snake coiling around its next meal.

"Hey, sweet darlin'. You didn't like my brother. Maybe you'll like me better."

The stench of his tobacco and whiskey-laced breath against the nape of her neck gagged her. His body touching hers repulsed her. Her eyes flashed. Every muscle in her body tensed. Her breathing stopped.

"Aww, leave her alone, Shaw," Liam said, "Can't you tell a lady when you see one?"

"Breathe Arose," Bessonth's voice repeated in her head, *"relax...find your center."*

"Shut up, Liam! Before I backhand ya!" Liam retreated up to the wall and twitched.

She closed her eyes and collected her composure, but the rush made her blood tingle. The element of surprise would be her best defense. She opened her eyes with renewed spirit.

Her left fist cracked the air in front of her. Her elbow snapped free.

"Wah?" Shaw said, startled.

Thrusting her elbow behind her, deep into his gut, she felt his ribs snap. A rush of air pierced his lips. Damaged, he would be easy to take down. She savored the moment of complete control.

She grimaced as she struck the bridge of his nose with the back of her hand. The bone crunched under her knuckles. He shrieked and fell to his knees. Blood gurgled in his throat and entered his lungs. He gasped for air. His hands covered his face. Thick crimson liquid poured from between his fingers.

With her assailant on the floor beaten, she anticipated a continued fight. She taunted Liam with a crook of her finger.

Liam froze. Confusion and panic filled his eyes. Liam shook his head and stared down at his brother, Shaw, on the floor still clutching his face. A smile briefly flashed across Liam face, before he turned to tend to his brother.

She adjusted her dress and gave him a slight bow of her head.

"Have a good day, young man," she said and continued on her way down the dusty street to the bookstore.

Once inside, she mixed in with patrons. Her eyes were glued to the door to see if anyone followed her in.

Shelves filled with books surrounded tables and benches, where customers read undisturbed. She nodded hello to the storekeeper, George, a balding, spectacled man in a white smock.

"*Bon jour*, Mademoiselle Du Mouchelle," he greeted her with a leer.

George's manner seemed out of place in a store of books and quiet reading. It seemed to Arose he hid behind his smock and half-moon glasses, as if he were in a costume. As she neared him, she could smell the salt and sea air that had been ground into his skin. His shoulders and arms were muscled in the way that only years of hard labor can develop.

George spied out the window, ducking as the watchman passed.

She had known the shopkeeper for only a few months. The previous owners had disappeared without a word. Whispers in town told of underworld goings on with the previous shopkeeper and his wife. The next day George had appeared.

"Pirates!" A voice yelled in her mind. Her skin tingled, and her eyes darted around the room. Her heart quickened at the thought. Arose knew how to discover more about this mystery; she could summon the power of the opalescent gem to take her to the astral plane where she could walk into George's past as an unseen ghost.

She found a quiet spot between the towering stacked shelves. Chatter from the customers in the store faded out as her body stood firmly planted on the slat wood floor of the bookstore. She willfully pushed her spirit out. A silver cord tied her essence to her mortal self. She moved as a disembodied spirit into the cloudless sky, pulling her far out toward the open ocean, further than she had ever been taken before. Seagulls screeched around her as she floated above an angry sea. Salt air filled her lungs, and she felt the mist against her face. In the distance, she saw the white sails of a large ship. She lingered high above the main sail, her gossamer form unseen.

High up in the sails, George swung from rigging to rigging. His spectacles and smock had been traded in for a first mate insignia on his sleeve and a dagger at his hip.

He shouted, "Aye, Cap'm St. James," to a dark figure below. She looked down to the shadowy figure while she floated high above. A man in silhouette stood below her, his hair whipping in the ocean wind.

The scent of his hair sweetly reminded her of happier times. Like cedar, citrus fruit and iron. She could almost taste the citrus fruit, smell the cedar, and feel coolness of the iron cannonballs. Bright red to deep violet filled his aura. The center was filled with black, a black deep as the ocean depths.

He captivated Arose. She felt she knew him, knew the mix of the colors in his soul. Her desire to see this mysterious man in shadow became overwhelming. She needed to dive into his eyes, rummage through his chest and devour his soul. She needed all of him, and now. Propelled by her desire, bordering on an insatiable lust, she moved closer until the figure almost came into view.

He turned his shadowy face, looking at the area where she floated. For a moment, she swore he saw her. Bright blue eyes, like those of a northern wolf, glowed from the black. He held his hand out toward her face, touching her ghostly cheek. She felt his touch, like feathers falling on her cheekbone, trickling down her neck.

She felt a warmth she had only experienced twice in her life. A warmth like this one was more of an emotion than a sensory touch. She could remember the first time she felt so warm and content. She had been swathed in a soft blanket, hummed to and rocked, a name—her name—spoken in a soft high-pitched tone. The next time she felt this way, a young man cradled her in his arms and delivered her to safety.

Arose reached her hand up to meet his. Their fingers mingled, intertwined. She closed her eyes. A pull at her shoulder broke their moment together. She turned to see the same demon who dragged her almost to the gates of hell. Gasping, she met his wide blank eyes. She pulled out a silvery blade and watched it pulse with energy.

Years of preparation with Bessonth had toughened her. She no longer feared the little demon, which surprised her more than it did him. Arose spun herself in a full circle, her long hair catching the air. The demon flipped back to avoid the slice, countering with a swipe of claw-like talons. Four red lines appeared across her forearm. Bringing her arm to her mouth, Arose tasted the iron in her own blood. The demon smiled and continued his attack. With a deep growl, it poised to jump at her.

Arose waved her hand. The little demon froze. Its feet were stuck in the clouds that surrounded them. She walked to it. Looking up at her glowing blade, the demon shook all over. She raised it over her head. The threat enough for the both of them, she willed the silver cord to pull her spirit back to her body. She snapped herself out of the vision with a shake of her head and looked down at her wounded arm. Healed and scarred as if they had always been there, she covered the deep lines with the frilled edge of her sleeve.

She pushed back the thoughts of the frightful creature and focused on her encounter with Captain St. James. Did he see her or feel her presence? She touched her cheek where his hand caressed her only moments before.

"How did he do that?" she whispered. A sudden feeling of foreboding came over her, like cold steel through her heart.

A pirate captain, and George, his first mate, she thought.

Danger, energy and excitement filled the Captain's aura. She couldn't help but wonder who and where he came from. She took a deep breath to clear her head and let out a heavy sigh.

She felt the shopkeeper's eyes on her as she once again breezed through the aisles of the bookstore. She touched a book here and there, tracing a finger up and down the book spines. His spellbound eyes followed from behind the bookshelves and peered at her from over the tops.

"Mademoiselle Du Mouchelle," he called to her in a thick French accent. "I have come into possession of a new book, *Histoire Comique*. It is in French. Please come and look."

She drew near to see the book in his hand. She inched close enough so he could whisper in her ear.

"*Français est la langue d'amour*. The language of love, Mademoiselle," he breathed.

Quick warmth came to her cheeks. She realized why he followed her. The thought made her shudder.

She placed the *Histoire Comique* under her arm for purchase.

"*Merci*," she said with a curtsy.

George stared at her for a moment with a haunting look. His eyes took in the curve of her mouth, tracing a line down her long neck to her décolleté'. He made a hasty retreat to the back room and closed the curtain. She sat for a short while to explore the book he offered her. She gathered her things for the long walk home.

Arose heard a crash. A moan come from the back room. She walked over to the doorway and pulled open the curtain.

"*Mes ye? Ou malad*?" she said in Creole. "Are you all right?"

She looked into the dusty air and saw George. He lay under a tumble of wooden crates. As the air cleared, she noticed an old brass telescope in his hand. Arose searched the room and found a hole in the wall, large enough for him to feed through the end of the telescope.

"Were you peeking through the scope?" she questioned. He sheepishly nodded.

"What were you looking at?"

He stared at her and held up a shaky hand. She followed his finger to where it pointed; it led straight to her bosom.

She let out a quick gasp, putting her hand over her

mouth; the book fell open on the ground. A watercolor of an unclad woman and man tangled in a carnal embrace stared up at her. She quickly looked away, and stepped back from the book, leaving it where it fell.

By now, customers clamored around. George moaned and let his head drop back to the crates. Two large men rushed toward him to help him to his feet. Arose turned and ran from the store.

Chapter Six
The Way Home

From the Astral Plane, the spirit of Arose Du Mouchelle watched at a distance while her living embodiment left the bookstore. She struggled to pass through the door while the townsfolk clamored their way in, some to help, some to gawk at the scene.

She found her horse, Duke, at the apothecary, where she'd left him tied. She watered him and led him to the edge of town. The road to the Du Mouchelle Plantation stood before her.

The spirit form Arose wished she could warn her embodiment of what would transpire, but she could not. She held her breath and waited to watch the events unfold.

Arose had to pass on the outskirts of the bog beyond the jumbie tree. Instead of riding the horse, she walked slowly, holding his reins, as he clopped down the road behind her. She looked to the sky. The sun had begun its descent into night. Since it must be around three, Arose hoped to return home in time for tea. Her stomach rumbled, and the only thing keeping her from grabbing some berries from the side of the road happened to be the corset her nanny, Domenga, had tied excessively tight in the morning.

Arose laughed when she thought of Domenga. Her nanny would shake her head and complain—life away from home had "ruined her for an hourglass figure" and insisted on squeezing the laces of the corset until her waist reached twenty-two and one-half inches.

Arose would just as soon go without it. It limited her agility—high kicks and flips were almost impossible to produce.

Her mother and sisters considered her unsuitable for marriage and way too bold for the vast majority of men. She usually agreed; she would have a problem being subservient to just any man.

Still, the vision from the bookstore stood out in her mind.

"Captain St. James." His name rolled off her tongue easily.

She wondered if he really saw her floating before him, or he could be reaching for a feather or some other flotsam crossing his path. No one else had ever been able to see her, no less touch her while in spirit form.

She imagined her fingers knuckle deep in his tousled light brown hair while her hand passed over a smooth chiseled chest. His well-muscled arm held her close while his hand caressed her cheek.

His eyes in a dancing crystal blue. They glared at her from under a furrowed brow. She sensed an ocean storm rising in them. A chill ran down her spine as she meandered down the deserted road, skirting the bog.

Deep in thought, Arose barely noticed the silence around her. Sounds of the bullfrogs and crickets were absent in the bog.

She inhaled deeply, trying to recapture the scent that came from his hair, but her throat closed. She gasped for air, putting her hand to her throat.

Duke whinnied and refused to walk any farther. She went to the saddle to mount the large horse. Her sight beginning to blur she could not find the stirrup to lift herself up. Holding fast to his reins while he bucked, his front hoof missed her head by inches. She made up her mind it would be better to let go of the tether. Duke bolted down the road.

Now alone, she covered her mouth and nose with the crook of her arm. Her lungs rejected the thick air. Arose coughed and fell to her knees. She looked up to the sky but only saw the sun's outline, blotted out by the smoke hanging in the air.

She had walked blindly into a poisonous brume. On her hands and knees, she stayed low until she found clean air, nearer to the ground.

Arose held her breath and tore off a strip of cotton from her skirt. By tying it around her nose and mouth, she could take a breath without choking. Her eyes stung, and her vision blurred. Wet soot streaked her face when she rubbed her watery eyes.

She did not know in which direction she was headed or where she should go. She crawled slowly, not wanting to gulp air. Shapes formed in fog-shadow ahead of her. She made her way toward them. She made a most horrible discovery.

She found the source of the thick brimstone. The dragon Bessonth, her friend and teacher, tail to neck sunk deep into the bog's soil. Only her head was visible, her jaws-wide amber eyes glazed over. From her mouth, deep blue fire shot into the sky.

Arose gasped, and quickly covered her mouth with a shaky hand. She turned away, as if not seeing it would make it less true. She bit her lower lip, angry with herself for allowing visions of St. James to cloud her mind.

Alive yet motionless, Bessonth did not struggle against her captivity, but seemed to accept her situation. Her light brown eyes followed a beautiful cloaked woman who emanated a low grumble. She circled the head of the dragon, tossing roots and herbs into her jaws which and sent sparks into the air as they burned. A large man stood near, as motionless as Bessonth. Mesmerized by the blue flame, he stared into it intently. Dread and fear surrounded the area.

Arose whispered to the Gem of the Red Spirit, *"Only dark magic could enslave a dragon. I feel Voodoo at work in this place. She must be a powerful priestess."* The stone warmed against her chest, answering her with a warning of danger.

She knew the area well; the downed trees were all too familiar. Where she stood should be mud and soupy leaves. Instead, the hard clay under her feet crackled as she stepped.

Arose held the Gem of the Red Spirit in her hand, crouched behind a dry tree, and vanished.

The cloaked woman threw a dried root into Bessonth's mouth. White-blue flames sputtered and flew high into the air. Intense heat lapped over Arose.

The woman spoke to the large man looming in the corner. "Look, Harold. Look into the dragon's fire."

Harold lumbered forward to Bessonth. Images appeared in the flames, first came Arose's father, next her mother, her sisters. They hovered above the fire, turning their heads to look at each other. They resembled living portraits hanging on the wall. Arose began to panic. She spun around, looking for the quickest way home.

The Priestess spoke to the childlike man. "There is the Du Mouchelle family. I have sent word to them with the arrangement of your marriage to their eldest daughter, and I added a little gift to make them a bit more than susceptible to my proposition. I sent a talisman which will spread a spell of oblivion to anyone near it."

Harold stared intently at the faces of the Du Mouchelle women, then turned to the priestess. "Sister, what will I get from this arrangement? I never planned to take a wife, Morel. Why would I get married?"

"Money, dear Harold, and lots of it. After you marry her, you will take the sugar plantation," she cooed at him. "Then we can make them all disappear!"

"Certainly you don't expect me to dirty my hands!" Harold spit back.

"Arose is there. You can make her do the dirty work." Morel smiled and carried on with her plan. "She could run the mill, and deal with the labor; after all, she is nearly one of them. She will be easily handled if you can get the Gem of the Red Spirit from her. She may even be convinced into ridding us of the rest of the family. With the Red Spirit attached to my heart and under my control, I can enter the Astral Plane and free the demons. The world can be ours. Everyone will bow to my will! And no one will be able to take it from me again!" Her guttural laugh went right through Arose. The Priestess's growing rage permeated the bog, increasing into a high-pitched crescendo.

Arose stood invisible in the shadows and looked into the swirling red opalescent gem. *"She is insane! She can't do that. Everyone will die."*

Harold smiled and nodded, clapped his hands, resembling a child.

"The girl, show me the girl, show me Arose. Morel! Please," Harold begged.

The woman hissed out a wicked laugh. "You want to see her? Do you, brother?"

Harold nodded as he stared into the flames. She tossed a handful of dust into the mouth of the beast. Blue flames sparked once again.

The outline of a female body appeared in the flames, naked and moving in a sultry dance. A white flame flickered off the top of her head while flaming hair blew around her face. Her hips swayed slowly side to side. White-hot flaming fingertips moved over her body. She ran them over her breasts and down her thighs.

Who is that? Arose thought. *Is she supposed to be me?* She looked down at her breasts, up again, and watched as her image gestured to Harold, taunting him.

"Oh, no, she is not..."

"Get me the Gem of the Red Spirit, Harold. After I open the gates of hell, I will return Arose to you. You can have her whenever you want!"

The flaming image of Arose stepped down from between Bessonth's jaws. Ivory skin appeared as it cooled. The hair turned long and sun-kissed, tumbled over her shoulders and down her back, her lips were full and blushed. A mirror image of Arose stood naked in front of Harold.

Arose watched silently, every nerve in her body twitching. Her skin crawled as if the centipedes had tunneled under her skin. She shuddered, her senses working against her.

"No!" she thought. She caught the word in her throat. They would find her quickly if she made a sound.

The nude imposter allowed Harold to take her in his arms. A rough hand pulled back her hair, lifting her face to reach his. He opened his large mouth to envelope hers.

Swallowing back the vomit when it reached her mouth, Arose couldn't help but made a hurling sound of "Gah!"

Her replica turned toward the disembodied sound. As a magical being, the image had the ability to see through the Gem of the Red Spirit's obscuring veil. Arose and her replica came eye to eye. The imposter screeched in horror at seeing her human embodiment and exploded back into blue flame from which she was formed. Harold pushed the smoldering carcass away while it's agonizing screams echoed through the bog. Flesh bubbled and burned from her body, crackled into shades of grey ash. White flame shot out of her eye sockets; her flowing hair singed and disappeared into dust. Acrid smoke coming from the fuming body smelled of the sharpness of burning human flesh. Pungent, dark smoke clung to Arose's nostrils, filling her lungs. She coughed and covered her face with the crook of her arm. Finally, the imposter's skull went shrieking back into the gaping mouth of the dragon and burst outward. Grey ash disappeared in the wind.

Harold grabbed at the flakes of ash as they blew away. Tears came to his eyes. Between sobs, he asked,

"Why, Morel? Why did you do that? Why did you make her go?" He fell to his knees, digging at the soil. He lifted lumps of dirt mixed with the imposter's ashes cupped in his hands. "Make her come back. Fix her."

Morel laughed wildly as she spoke. "I didn't kill your toy, Harold, the girl did it. She is near. The opalescent gem is trying to hide her from us, but she gave herself away."

Harold turned and squinted into the fog. "Where is she? I will kill her!" He spun around looking for the invisible Arose. "I don't see anyone."

"You will find her, Harold." Morel pulled a black vial out of her cloak and held it in the air.

"No, Morel. Don't do it," Harold begged. "Not again!"

"Find her, Harold! Without the Gem of the Red Spirit, she can be yours! She will be flesh and blood, the real body, the real soul." She opened the vial and poured it into the fire. The huge ball of flame flew into the air, scorching everything surrounding it.

Arose covered her face with her arm. A ghastly scream came from the man. When the smoke and fire cleared, Harold had disappeared. Arose scanned the area.

How could he have moved out of the way so quickly?

From directly in front of her came a noise low to the ground.

Hooves clacked along the hard clay. A grunt and a snort came from the huge boar before her; it planted its flat wet nose to the dry ground. Large tusks curled from its mouth. It sniffed until it caught a scent, which it followed around in circles, stopped. Harold, transformed into the huge boar, stared at the tree where she stood.

The amulet heated.

The charging animal crashed through fallen branches and roots standing in its path.

"He can smell me!" Arose leaped straight into the air and landed softly on a branch twenty feet up.

From her vantage point, she could see the very top of the jumbie tree in the distance.

The large beast held his head down and circled the ground below where Arose hid in the branches. It buried its long tusks deep under the shallow roots. It lifted its heavy head. She jumped to the next tree. Arose felt a tug, but hung onto the trunk.

The stiff branches of the falling tree caught her skirt, tearing it off. The blue and white lace skirt lay visible on top of the fallen tree.

The boar stepped over to the skirt and snorted it greedily. Arose's clever mind worked quickly. Now unencumbered by the extra fabric, she jumped a few trees closer toward the edge of the bog.

Harold ran in circles, relentlessly grunting and squealing.

Her home's rooftop peaked over the high canopy in the distance. Her corset would be the next to go.

She untied it quickly, ripping the satin laces through the grommets. She finally pulled it off her body. Her breasts fell free. She smelled it. Only the slight scent of lavender soap and the damp mustiness of her perspiration were on it.

She mustered up all her strength and flung it as far as she could. The beast caught the scent of it on the wind and ran over to where it fell.

It inhaled the scent from the corset deeply. Grabbing it by his teeth, he flung it back and forth over its head and fell to the ground, exhausted. Flat out in front of him, the corset laid in a pile of brown grass. He grunted, putting his nose into it. He stuck out his long black tongue and licked the material.

Arose crinkled her nose up into her forehead.

"Eww. What is he doing?"

His breathing came more rapid, lolling over to lay on his back. Snorting and sputtering, he rubbed against the bodice. She couldn't help her urge to laugh when a guffaw bubbled out of her throat. The Harold-beast groaned. Arose stood, close to a narrow escape, but a voice came from directly below. The priestess Morel had found her. Her laughter had given her away.

"Here she is!" she croaked, pointing out Arose's exact location in the tree.

Morel ran back toward the large beast, still rolling around on top of her bodice. Arose had only one article of clothing left. She stepped out of her pantaloons and tossed them high into the air. The breeze caught them, and they billowed like a sail. The woman ran toward the beast as the pantaloons followed in her wake. They closed in, fast.

Arose turned and leaped into the jumbie tree as the pantaloons landed squarely on Morel's shoulders. Arose did not look back. She jumped out of the tree and ran, completely naked, into the tall brown bushes.

From behind her in the bog, she heard Morel wail.

"No, no! You dumb beast! Let me go! Stop!" she screamed.

Arose sped toward her house and hopped in through the window to her room.

Chapter Seven
The Dinner Guest

Arose sat on her bed, trying to catch her breath. She looked up into the full-length mirror and frowned as she passed her hands over her hair, tied up so elaborately earlier in the day, now nappy from sweat and swamp water. Dirt and soot streaked her face.

She looked into the mystic opalescent gem. Its colors shifted uneasily. Arose moved closer to the mirror and stared into the morphing gem. She had never seen it behave so strangely. Red and orange flashed, faded to black.

She looked around. Her whitewashed walls were almost empty and plain, except for the fresco on one wall. Red flags flew on the tall masts high above a pitching sea. Arose had painted it from memory, soon after her return from her Uncle Edmund's ship.

On the dresser sat a bowl of water and the washcloth from her morning bath.

"Thank goodness Libby doesn't keep up with her chores." The cold water felt good on the scratches and bumps on her arms and legs. She cleaned off the soot and wet her hair through.

The whalebone comb tore through her tangled blonde mess and lavender soap swept away the smell of the swamp water. She put on a white lacy dressing gown and sat down on the bed, trying to decide the best way to warn her family of the imminent danger.

The image of Bessonth trapped underground played over in her head. How could Morel trap a dragon as strong and clever as Bessonth? Arose could not shake the feeling she somehow could be responsible for this. She held the opalescent gem tightly in her hand and spoke directly to it, "I'm worried for her too. I can free her, but I will need your help."

With those words, the spirit seemed to calm, the color shifts slowed. It remained warm to the touch, until a knock came at the door. It sprang back to life, glowing orange for an instant, and turned completely black.

"Rosie? Are you in there?" Her sister, Anne, called through the door.

Arose bit her bottom lip. Should she mention her encounter? If so, what should she say?

"Yes, Anne," she answered reluctantly. "Come in."

Anne entered the room. Her high collar skimmed the bottom of her chin. The dress's creamy white lace was almost indiscernible from the skin of her neck. Her black hair was pulled back severely—curls dripped off each side of her face. Very pretty in her own right, but she and Arose shared little resemblance.

"Anne? Can I speak with you?"

Anne leaned back on the door, her arms folded over her chest. She stared at Arose, already frustrated with the conversation.

Arose chose her words carefully. "I have a bad feeling. Someone is coming to endanger our family."

"What danger? You and your premonitions. I truly wish you would stop."

"Did a letter come for Fiona?"

"Yes, a proposal from a suitor. How did you know?"

Arose opened her mouth to speak, but Anne put her hand up to silence her. "Never mind, you are just envious. She has a suitor and you don't."

"No…listen to me…" Arose shook her head and her words trailed off.

"The supper table is set. Mother wants you to come to eat."

Anne turned her back to Arose and walked down the hall to the dining room. Arose followed.

As soon as she entered the dining room, dizziness and nausea overcame her. The floor moved under her feet, and she staggered.

Lady Katherine looked disappointed as Arose entered the room.

"Rosie, are you still in your dressing gown? Have you been at the rum again? Go dress properly for supper."

As was customary, Arose stood behind her chair and waited for her father to enter the room.

Glistening pewter platters set around the table were filled with potatoes and several small pheasants. A large pitcher filled with spiced mead sat in the center of a laurel wreath. A brightly colored pottery bowl filled with apples, mangos, and grapes from the arbor adorned the table. The grapes spilled over its edge and draped delicately onto the embroidered tablecloth.

"Mother, I have something to talk to you and Father about before dinner."

Lady Katherine ignored her.

"Arose, we have a guest for supper, a guest who will soon become a member of the family." Katherine continued, "Your father is making arrangements at this very moment! Mr. Ambrielle has not only agreed to take Fiona's hand in marriage, but to take over the sugar plantation as well."

Anne spoke up to add to the argument. "You know Father has been sick and cannot run things as he once did."

Arose took a deep breath. "This person is not who he appears to be."

Lady Katherine's face went bright red.

"No dear, simply not possible. We have known the Ambrielle family for years. You remember his sister, Marie. Marie Ambrielle." She looked at her daughter's puzzled expression. "When she married the Reverend Murphy, she changed her name to Mary. Mary Murphy, Arose? Don't you remember her?"

Stumped for a moment, Arose did not believe her ears and to top off her confusion the woozy feeling grew worse. Her tongue felt stilted, and she struggled to talk.

"M-M-M-Mary M-M-Murphy?" Arose stammered, trying to make sense of the revelation.

The pit of her stomach began to turn and she tasted bile in her mouth.

Could pious Mary Murphy be the Voodoo priestess, Morel?

She stared blankly at her, after a moment realizing Morel had cast a Spell of Oblivion; the talisman must be somewhere in the room. Even worse, now the spell attempted to attach itself to her. Lady Katherine would not or could not remember the past. In particular, she did not remember how, as a child, Arose ran home in tears after they hunted her down in the bog. How the Vicar and Mary Murphy wanted to subject her to the trials by ordeal that would have meant her death.

Certainly, under the shadow of a spell, her home tried to poison her mind. Making it all the worse, someone or something wanted to stop her from speaking. Cramps in her womb doubled her over. The Gem of the Red Spirit burned against her chest, doing its best to repel the evil magic. She struggled to remain under her own control, but didn't know how much longer she could hold out.

The sound of laughter came from the glass arboretum. Her father clapped a tall man on the back as they walked to the house.

Harold Ambrielle looked different from when she saw him in the bog. So different, in fact, Arose began to doubt herself. This could not be the same person. He changed into a beast and chased her through the bog. His neatly combed dark hair was shining with oil, and his genial smile and a pleasant demeanor charmed the entire family. All fooled except for her; she saw it as a mask. Underneath, his grotesqueness lingered.

It's the spell. The spell gets worse the longer I stay in here. Morel said she sent a wedding gift, a Talisman that would hold the spell. What is it?

The room grew blurry as she scanned the table. She tried to move, but her legs were lead weights, anchoring her to the floor.

"Look, they are approaching—too late. You can't leave the room now." her stepmother said, adjusted her face to a skewed smile and beamed at them as they stepped down the breezeway. The chair before Arose became her crutch, holding so tightly to its spindles her fingers blanched. Her eyes glazed over, white blinders covered them, she was seeing through a muslin weave.

Harold Ambrielle and her father clamored into the dining room. Laughter and camaraderie ensued, seeming like old chums rather than new acquaintances. Her sister, Fiona, trailed silently behind, her head held low. Fiona, a frail girl, had an air of polite obedience from years of polish her mother had applied to her personality. The innocence in her eyes made her appear years younger than Arose, even though she was five years older.

Her father's smile faded when he spotted his daughter wearing the sheer dressing gown, while a leer emerged from Ambrielle.

Without warning, a vision took over her mind; her head hit the wall. The wind quickly knocked out of her lungs. A hand clutched her throat. Ambrielle's large body pressed the air further from her.

"Where is it... where is the stone?" His growl, somewhere between human and the boar he had transformed into, wafted across her mind. She started to black out, her knees folding under her. As if in a dream, she pushed the air before her, fighting for her life against someone that was not there.

"Arose? Are you all right?" Lady Katherine gasped, her eyes shifting between the struggling girl and Ambrielle.

"Mr. Ambrielle, please excuse our daughter, she must be feeling ill." Turning to Arose, Lady Katherine whispered so no one could hear, "Go to your room and lie down."

Arose nodded and stumbled into the hall. Her bare feet dragged down the corridor, using the wall more than once to keep from dropping to her knees.

She managed to make it to her chambers and fell on the bed. Her thoughts began to clear. *The talisman Morel sent must be in the dining room.*

While in the house, the talisman had the power to take the opalescent gem and her mind.

Chapter Eight
A Night Out As Evan

Arose lay on the bed exhausted. She waited for her second sight to speak to her. She sat up and collected all her strength. She called out "Bessonth! Can you hear me?" She waited for a moment. Nothing came to her. Not even a whisper from her dear Bess. She collapsed back onto her small white sheeted bed, and fell into a deep sleep.

Her mind spun as she dove into a misty dream. Her mind's eye followed muddy feet as they ran through the bog. The squeals of a screeching boar echoed around her. Slipping, she fell to the ground while mud, flung into the air, fell into her hair like mossy rain. She crawled on her hands and knees until she found a hiding place behind a sandy dune of a cliff. She looked around desperately and reached down to her chest for the help of the amulet. When she reached for it, it would fade out, and return when she removed her hand.

On a cliff, the ocean rose and fell below her. She dove deep into it.

Under water, bubbles drifted around her. She looked up to the surface, circling over the water; a winged dragon cast her shadow.

Bessonth! She is free!

She smiled widely and swam up. When she hit the air, she awoke.

Arose shot up out of the bed and shook off the spell of oblivion like a heavy cloak. She remembered everything.

Bessonth waited, buried neck deep in the bog, and the talisman hid somewhere in the dining room and she knew the man, sitting in her home, to be married to her sister—was the enemy.

Arose sat on the bed and put her head into her hands. Tears welled up in her eyes, as she thought of her dear sweet Bessonth, so helpless. Morel's captive. She did not wait for her tears to fall. Rather, she straightened up and gathered her courage. She would not crumble, not raise the white flag of defeat.

The spirit Arose watched her past self with pride. She realized her trip into her history was almost at an end.

She snatched the brown leather satchel from under the bed. In it, she found an oversized black shirt, trousers and riding boots. She dressed in a flurry and wrapped a long gauzy strip of linen tightly around her breasts. The Gem of the Red Spirit pressed to her skin. The baggy shirt would hide whatever curves would tell the tale of her womanhood. She completed her transformation by slicking her blonde locks back with a green ribbon. She grabbed her scabbard, which held a gleaming sabre; lastly, she shoved a dagger into her boot.

Arose lifted her leg over the windowsill and ran through the sugar cane to the open field. The sun, just about to set, turned the clouds a purplish pink. She sat on the sand wondering how she could escape her troubles. She traced the initials—NDM—engraved into the blade, the only remnants of her given name she hated since her youth. Nessarose.

Shouts on the wind and the jangle of chains alerted her while Harold mounted the stallion, Duke. The chase commenced and Ambrielle would never take no for an answer. She hid behind a mound of sand. He passed her by, taking the road into Montego Bay.

She took the Gem of the Red Spirit out of its hiding place and thought of Bess, captured and held underground, forced to do Morel's bidding.

Arose closed her eyes and began a soul walk into the past. She watched herself as a young child running to the bog with Josiah, Simon, and Leon trailing behind. Her heart ached for Old Bess, accused of witchcraft, as she turned into the Blue Fire Dragon.

Unseen, she stood behind the gangly young man holding the reins of a large black horse. The name "Blaze" echoed after her father spoke it. She cheered when Bessonth found her imprisoned, high above the Sea of Marmara.

Her smile turned to anger when she came upon the mighty dragon buried up to her neck in the bog.

With her bittersweet voyage to the past over, her essence pulled back to her mortal self. She took a cleansing breath and came back to the present, her trip into the Astral Plane looping into the current moment.

Her ghostly spirit joined her mortal body and she sat once again on the sandy dune looking out to the sea. The pendant in her hand. Its silver cord invisibly entwined her heart.

She stood, brushed the sand from her buttocks, and placed the pendant between her skin and the linen and pressed in as Bess had done to seal the bond. Arose took one last look at the ships in the harbor.

Run, yes, she could run, but there were a few things to take care of first.

A reenergized Arose trotted into the town she had left that very afternoon, dreaming of the mysterious Captain St. James. So much had taken place in the day. She still had to devise a plan.

Josiah, Simon, and Leon! She would enlist their help, but they still did not know the identity of their friend Evan. She would have to break it to them, gently.

Arose entered the town, looking for her three friends. Since it was the end of the week, they most probably were in one of the taverns spending their pouches of gold, or maybe in an alleyway shooting the loaded die Josiah usually kept for a fixed game.

Arose found them in the Raven's Nest, a murky

tavern on the docks of Montego Bay. When she entered, the smell of stale ale and tobacco stung her nose. The tavern wench smiled when she passed, trying to catch her attention. A poker player leaned his chair back, trying to keep his cards out of sight from the other players, holding them close to his chest, even though he shifted uneasily in his seat trying to sneak a peek at his neighbor's hand.

She scanned the area, memorizing the room—the faces of the patrons, where they stood and what they were engaged in.

Josiah, Simon, and Leon sat at a table to the left of the door, two tables in with one table behind them. She took note of how many steps it took to walk to the table, twenty-four in all.

Taking the chair closest to the main beam, she swung her leg over the back. Her entrance caught many eyes. She tried to become less conspicuous by motioning to the server for a pint.

"Evan!" Josiah paused for dramatic effect. He clasped her arm and slammed her on the back, a manly greeting she had become accustomed to. "Listen, we have a plan. We will be rich!"

"Another plan? Don't include me in your schemes, Josiah."

"Aye, Evan. This is the big one," whispered Leon. "We won't have to scrape for the old man anymore."

"Scrape?" Arose lifted her eyebrows in disbelief. "The poor man gives you a farthing a week, and you barely do a thing for him. 'Cept rob him blind and sleep all day under the mimosa tree. Fine lot you are."

Simon's voice boomed over the din of the tavern. "Hey. How would you know, Evan? I never saw you at the Cinnamon Bay Plantation." Some of the patrons quieted and looked their way,

Leon added softly, "The only one I see come and go is the Du Mouchelle girl. She brings baskets of food each

week for the ole man."

Josiah smiled widely. "Awe yea, Arose Du Mouchelle, did you see the pomegranates on that girl?" He nodded, holding his hands over his chest exaggerating the size of her breasts.

The three friends bantered back and forth; Arose smiled and took her sword out of its scabbard. Embarrassed, but even though they were talking about her feminine attributes, they no longer focused on Evan's absence from the plantation. She twirled the sharp end of her sword into the wood plank between her feet.

"We knew her, Evan, back when she ran with us. A wild, mop-haired child, she could swim like no other. She climbed trees and swam with us as naked as the day she was born," Josiah reminisced. He pointed at Leon. "Remember the time she saved you from drowning? She kept telling you not to pass the breakers, but you did anyway, and there she came out of the water, dragging you ashore, and you, limp as a rag doll. Almost as if she knew what would happen."

Leon nodded in agreement with a silent smile.

Simon spoke with an effeminate twang.

"She came back in all white lace and fine frills." He held his arm out daintily as if he held an imaginary handkerchief in his sausage-like fingers.

The members of the table broke out into riotous laughter. He cleared his throat and his voice went deep again. "No way would she give her old friends a second glance."

Arose smiled, looking down at the hole she drilled into the plank.

"No, my boys, my brothers, I can never forget you."

"Just about when you came to town, Evan. Strange, huh?" Leon stared at Arose intently for a moment. Their eyes met when a quizzical look came over Leon's face.

Josiah broke the uncomfortable silence. "I hear she

took down the Murphy boys today."

"They were getting a bit too friendly, and she bloodied Shaw Murphy's nose." Simon laughed.

Arose thought back to her youth and remembered the cruel bullies she'd repeatedly protected the boys from. Shaw, older than they by more than ten years, would hold Simon's arms back, while Faolan would beat his large belly until the boy fell to the ground in tears. With Harold as their uncle, they would be in-laws to her sister. Her blood ran cold when she thought of the plantation workers and what kind of taskmaster Shaw Murphy would be. In her head, she heard Domenga's grandson Jessup scream as a lash cracked. She turned her head and shivered until the screams faded.

Arose saw an opportune time to admit to her friends that she had pretended all this time to be their friend Evan. She leaned forward and beckoned them to come closer. They gathered around. Arose opened her mouth to speak in a hushed tone. "I am—"

Someone bumped her shoulder.

Looking up, she saw the large hindquarters of a short man in a high powdered wig. He wore a pink long coat, lace cuffs dripping over his pudgy fingers.

The man looked down at her when she looked up. Many times, she caught the eye of men who looked for handsome young company. He appraised her face.

"You have finely chiseled cheek bones and lovely golden-green eyes. Charles Wooster at your service, young man," he said with a slight bow. "I saw you from the corner of the bar and I just had to meet you."

Angered by the interruption at such a crucial time, she stood up, a head taller than the older gentleman. "'Pardon me' should have been your first words," she said in her deep Evan voice.

"I cannot be pardoned, because pardons are for accidents. And my bumping you could not be called an

accident," the little man drawled.

"I suggest you should just be on your way," Arose commanded.

The little man fluttered a white hanky trimmed in lace over her face. Arose seethed, but the man withdrew his hanky and sauntered away. The moment lost, Arose sat again to rejoin the noisy conversation her cohorts were engrossed in.

Laughter and shouts came from every end of the bar. Tension grew in the unruly crowd. Voices darted in and out of her consciousness. She blocked them out; she wanted... she needed another chance to speak to the boys.

The door opened, the crowd grew with travelers. The bar's prime location made it an easy mark for those who disembarked from ships landing at the pier. Anabel bustled passed a shoulder high tray of beer mugs, filled to their brims. The new patrons filled the already crowded tavern; at the bar customers stood three rows deep to get a pint. The smell of unwashed bodies and stale cigar smoke filled the air.

She felt a nudge once again. When she turned, she saw the little man had returned, and this time he brought reinforcements.

A tall thin man now stood looking down at her. He had a long face and crooked nose. His greenish complexion made him look as if he had been sick recently.

"Yes, I see, Charles. He has a fine handsome face. Nevertheless, what of his physique? You know I appreciate broad shoulders and a taut stomach."

Arose rolled her eyes. Josiah spoke up to the men. "Come on gents. Can't a man have a pint with some friends?"

Simon stood and put his hand on Arose's shoulder. "Be on your way, he's not interested."

Frustrated, Arose slammed her sword into its scabbard.

"Come Roger, he is obviously already taken." The small man said to his cohort. He glanced at Simon and down at his hand, still on Arose's shoulder. A sly smile spread across his pallid face. Simon quickly retracted his hand, blushing.

The group sat in uncomfortable silence for a moment. Arose took a large mouthful of ale and slammed the cup on the table. She would have to bring the conversation back around.

"Tell me about your idea, Josiah. What is the big plan?"

Josiah stood and waved his hands in the air, looking left and right and behind himself. They all followed his lead, looking around for eavesdroppers.

He leaned in and beckoned them to come closer. "Well, you know the tall ship, the Red Spirit?" He paused and waited for her to nod.

With one eyebrow lifted, she shook her head no.

"No? Where you been all this time, Evan?"

"Busy…I have been very busy," she said deeply.

"Get with the times, man!" Simon laughed.

Josiah continued, "The ship is here to get five hogsheads of pure cane from the Du Mouchelle Plantation." Hearing her plantation mentioned made her uncomfortable. She stared intently at Josiah waiting for him to convey the rest of their scheme.

"Well, the plan is," —he leaned in and beckoned again to his friends—"we are going to plunder the barrels in the Port of San Sabastian, before it returns to the Red Spirit. And get this…" He paused. "I made a still! We can have our own rum made in a matter of days!" He laughed, very proud of himself, a toothy grin plastered on his face.

Her big chance had come! Determined to tell them, she stood to make her declaration. She stopped in mid-motion when jostled once again. Hard. She bumped the table and spilled her ale on the floor. Broken glass crunched

under her feet.

She stared out to the distance, the fire growing in her belly. Charles and Roger again! She readied to take the little man and heave him out the door. She blindly pushed back.

Connecting her shoulder with a large mass behind her caused a chain of events she wished she hadn't started.

It began with a deep voice, who, taken unawares, cried out with a large "ooph," after which came the distinct noise of poker chips and gold coins hitting the floor. Anabel screamed when the tray she balanced came crashing down, the sound of tables and chairs simultaneously being scraped along the wooden floor while people stood to avoid the shards of glass and ale flying everywhere. All this gave her the feeling she had just caused Armageddon.

Wincing, she turned to see a large man spread out over the poker table, the playing cards and gold scattered all around. The players tried to gather their gold as fights rang out when some were taking more than their share. The whores were on their hands and knees shoving gold into their cleavages. The man whose body covered the green felt poker table stood up, flailing his arms to gain his footing.

"Who pushed me?" he bellowed. His accent proclaimed his Bow-bell low end, Cockney roots. All fingers pointed at Arose.

The man turned to look behind him.

Arose's eyes widened. She recognized his face. Harold Ambrielle furrowed his heavy brow. His demeanor, quite a bit less gentlemanly than before, looking more akin to the man who chased her down in the bog rather than the cultured squire she met at home.

He stared Arose down. Her best defense would be a speedy exit. She formulated her escape: grapple the rafter over Ambrielle's head and swing close enough to make her way out the door, or she hoped it would turn out somewhat the same. More men surrounded her the longer she stood there, and being surrounded there would be nowhere else to go—but up. The Gem of the Red Spirit burned in warning under the tight linen wrap.

"Hey, you…boy! You pushed me!" His finger pointed down to the center of her face. Her eyes crossed as she looked down at the finger almost touching her nose. Although she knew full well a bar brawl could easily ensue, a toothy grin came to her face, overjoyed by the fact that he didn't recognize her.

She had to catch him off guard. Using some quick thinking, she put a foot squarely on the seat next to her. With a hop, she stepped up onto Harold's shoulder and leaped to the closest beam. Using the momentum, she swung as hard as she could through the air. She somersaulted and landed near the door, but not near enough.

With Ambrielle leading, several of the men rushed toward her, halted. Closing in, they began to laugh. They shared toothless smiles as Arose backed closer to the door.

She pulled her gleaming sword from its sheath, pointing it at the determined crowd.

From the back of the room, a cloaked man ran toward her. The brim of a plumed hat hid most of his face. A beard covered his chin, accenting a strong jaw and supple lips.

He brushed past her and blocked her way out of the door. A gust of wind brought his scent to her nose.

Cedar and iron! St. James? she thought.

Her eyes narrowed and she attempted to look under the wide brimmed hat.

"Move away from the door!" she demanded. The man shook his head and refused to move. "Don't make me fight you. I will win," she said assuredly. Her razor sharp foil pointed directly at him. He said nothing, and deftly pulled out his sword.

Shocked when, only able to make out a blur of steel,

the man ripped the sword from her grasp. No one had ever disarmed her before! The sword flew into the air and he caught it in mid-flight. The lips beneath the wide brim smiled playfully.

"Well, maybe not," she said under her breath. Disarmed, Arose looked for her next escape. The door stood within reach, blocked only by the caped obstacle. She squelched her gut instinct to grab the heating opalescent gem and disappear from sight. But that could lead to her being tied to a witch's stake for the ultimate *auto-da-fe'*.

From the corner of her eye, she saw the glint of her steel sword. She raised her hand and caught it by the hilt. She smiled and squatted low. The man came up beside her and stood at her side. She looked up, trying to spy his face under the shadow of the hat. He dipped the brim lower.

A throaty growl came from Ambrielle. She gasped and turned back to the growing crowd of men behind them. The group laughed and egged them on. A young one rushed them and attempted to cleave her over her head.

Her steel clanged, blocking two sloppy blows from an inebriated sailor. The man hit the ground and crawled under a table to sit with a forgotten brown bottle. Simon, standing on the table, threw his large body on a group of five men, felling them all to the ground. Josiah went to each, pulling at their shirts and knocking them out with a punch to the jaw or sent them hopping with a stomp on their foot.

Leon took complete advantage of the confusion to crawl to each, removing their coin bags while they were not looking.

"Yeaaahhhh!" yelled the crowd of men as they attacked.

She whirled around as she blocked quick thrusts. Her new partner flung off his cape, covering the faces of some would-be attackers. They fought side by side, sometimes back to back, blocking and stabbing while the mob attacked. Her comrade laughed, while attackers fell to the floor, bloodied and screaming for a scratch. She struck out with her leg when she found an opening and watched a man tumble down holding his scrotum.

They moved closer to the door with every stroke. It flew open as if a gust of wind had taken it. He pulled off the wide brimmed hat and flung it into the crowd as a diversion. Taking the bait, like a shark after minnows, the crowd tumbled after the expensive chapeau. He grabbed her by the wrist and pulled her out into the street.

"Follow me!" he shouted to her.

The two ran through the streets. The man's soft leather coat fluttered as he led her up the paved road to the edge of town. Ambrielle and the crowd yelled curses and took chase.

The stranger watched her profile as she jaunted over rocks large enough to confound even the best runner. The rush of blood to her lips made them pinker. He smiled "You quite ready to be rid of them?"

"Yes!" she panted. "I can't... quite take... a full breath."

He took a chance to look into her shirt as the wind billowed it. There they were; the linen bindings that fooled all present into thinking this "she" would be a "he."

He nodded, "At the turn of the road! Be prepared to jump into the shoal."

Her breasts strained against their bindings. The opalescent gem burned into her chest.

The mob followed far behind, but their lead would dwindle if she could not loosen the bindings. They reached the end of the town and leaped over an embankment.

Falling behind the sandy hill, they ducked low. The stranger snuck a quick look over the peak.

Ambrielle and the mob ran past.

Arose tried to catch enough breath to fill her lungs, but her bound breasts would not let her inhale deeply.

Dizziness swam in her head while the burning opalescent gem singed her skin.

Her eyes could not focus enough to make out her accomplice's face. He turned away and watched as the crowd ran toward the bog.

"Who are you?" she asked, her head spinning.

As all light dimmed for her, he turned and said, "St. James, Captain St. James."

Chapter Nine
Breakfast Aboard the Red Spirit

June 6, 1692

"St. James. Captain St. James." The voice echoed in a dream. She saw a shaded face approach her, her body lifted. Cradled deep in the safety of strong arms, she tried to open her eyes but her head pounded so much she decided to keep them closed.

When she did open her eyes, billows of cool white surrounded her. Perched in a chair beside her, a man snored loudly, his head back. His large boots crossed over and up on the bed where she sat. Her center started to ache. She thought of how liquid his movements were. How each movement, once begun, tumbled imperceptibly to the next, cascading as water would over rocks in a stream. His devilish smile when he disarmed her in the tavern. How he protected her even as the mob moved in. She wanted him; she wanted his strong arms around her.

Her pearlescent spirit floated out of her body. It sailed through the air to where he slept. Hovering over him, her ghostly hand passed up his chest and into his hair. The strands twisted around her fingers as if they were alive. She pulled his face up to look at her, yanking his hair so that he let out a small gasp of surprise and pleasure. A shadowy mask over his nose and eyes hid his face from her in the darkness. She ran her hands down his thick shoulders entwining his fingers with hers. She lifted his hands and placed them on her full hips. Leaning down, she brought her lips to his, kissing him with the light touch of a feather. His body moved under hers and she tugged at the wrappings that bound her breasts.

She felt the cold of steel pressed against her skin and with a slice, the wrappings fell to the floor. Now, with her breasts free, she covered his face in them holding his head against her pearlescent skin.

She sat facing St. James, her weightless body bestrode him, while he held her firmly, passing his lips over her invisible skin, his tongue leaving liquid lines where they passed. Down her neck to her nipples, he sucked and tugged at the iridescent pinkish orbs.

His hardness touched her and she arched her back. He hissed out a moan of enjoyment entering her. Her ghostly sighs reverberated in the darkness, her spirit body rising and falling in the air. He held her shimmering essence before him, passing his hands over her skin, his hands finally resting on her hips. The motion she initiated was taken over by his masculine thrusts, his grip tightening around her. He lifted her up and down, his body helpless but to enjoy the sensations. In her dream, reckless abandon washed over her. Her eerie gasps were joined by his quickened breaths; he thrust and moaned one last time, as they found euphoria simultaneously. She leaned down and kissed him sweetly, allowing herself to linger there, while she shivered the last of her orgasm in his arms. Her dream-self floated with a whoosh back to her earthbound body. She felt herself fall against the coolness of the downy quilt and drifted into yet another colorful dream.

Arose woke the next morning with a dull ache in her head and cotton in her mouth. Exhausted from chasing her fantasies all night, she closed her eyes and placed her hands over her head. She remembered her dream clearly, the sight of the large boots on her bed, the cold steel against her flesh. The moans of excitement she and St. James shared.

"Captain St. James," she cooed with a smile, biting into her lower lip. She drawled it low and deep, the way she would utter it if his ear would be within reach of her lips. The thought titillated her, but it happened only in her dream.

Arose lay on her stomach, her hair fallen over her face. Half buried into the downy pillow, she could barely see over a mountain of white linen and red silk.

She reached up and placed her hand on the billowy fluff in front of her. Her hand sank into a heap of a goose down quilt. A large dark headboard stood sentinel over her. At each corner of the bed were tall-spindled posters. They reached up to a canopy just below the beamed ceiling, from which hung a fringed red tapestry. She climbed up to her knees to inspect the intricately carved headboard. She ran her fingers over the curves of a black rosette.

"Ebony," she whispered, and whistled softly. She lifted her eyes to look around the room. At the far end, a huge wardrobe stood sentry. A window sat high above the floor. The plush chair, where in her dream St. James slept, sat empty, pushed against the wall in the far corner.

She had not seen much of luxury since her uncle returned her to Jamaica. It felt wonderful to be in such rich surroundings again. She spread her arms and fell back onto the feather bedding.

A cool salty breeze gently caressed her bare nipples. The smell of Captain's skin still clung to her. Draping her face with St. James's shirt collar, she took a deep breath and lingered in his scent. Her moment of sheer joy turned to anguish as she curled up in pain that emanated from her womb. She gasped for air and put her hand to her chest. She found it empty, and felt the emptiness of her once full heart. She gazed downward to where her shirt and her binds should be hiding the powerful opalescent gem. All she saw were the pink peaks of her breasts. It couldn't be gone! Her disbelief kept her searching her neck.

The linen wrappings lay on the floor, sliced in two. The dream she had the night before flashed through her mind, but the feeling there had to be something more egged her on. She held her searing gut, her hands shaking; the heat of tears came to her eyes.

She leaped off the bed and felt around her chest, inside her shirt and around her back. She looked down to her chest; there where the Gem of the Red Spirit would be, a red mark sat. She touched it. The feather light silver cord sparkled while it twisted about her fingers and disappeared.

The stone had never left her neck, not even once in ten years. Somehow they were still connected. The small hairs on her arms raised and she panted uncontrollably. She was unable to catch her breath, and her head swam.

She tore the covers from the bed, searching for her prized possession. Feather pillows hit the floor as she passed her hand under the linen sheets.

Crawling on her hands and knees, she frantically searched the room,

"Please, oh please!" she breathed. "That blaggard! He stole it! He kidnapped the Red Spirit and stuck me out on the ocean!"

Arose crawled until she reached the far end of the room and climbed up on the plush chair. The first morning beams of light became brighter as they streamed into the room through the pane glass window. She passed her hand over every inch of the windowpane, perhaps to find it in some remote corner of the room.

A seagull screeched outside the window. She focused as she blinked out into the red morning sun. Way out in the distance, the shoreline of Montego Bay bobbed in and out of sight through the paned glass and ocean, plenty of it, between her and the land. It would take her half the day to get back home. She probably would arrive late for Fiona's wedding, if she made it at all. Joy bubbled up in her and a moment of peace spread over her like a cool breeze.

She had escaped; she would have no more work, no

more toil on the plantation, no longer chased after by Ambrielle. But the notion quickly came to an end, she would also have no more power, no Bessonth to lean on, no more happiness of watching the children of the servants run and play within the flowers she had planted.

A weak knock came from the carved wood door. She spun around to face the sound, her peaks popping out of the shirt.

"Who is it?" She ran over to the bed and snatched the sheet up to cover her bare chest.

The voice that came from the other side of the door sounded weak and nervous. "It's Reggie. I... I... I... have come with a bit of breakfast for ya."

Her stomach grumbled; she had left home before supper, her share of the spiced roast most likely given to the dogs.

"Come in."

Reggie, an old man with white hair and little round spectacles, shuffled in. His large belly fell over the top of his britches. He carried a sterling silver tray with a cup for tea; steaming water in a flowered ceramic pot sat next to it. There were fresh oranges and a breakfast casserole. In the corner of the tray, a rose sat—a creamy yellow, the tips of the petals looked as if they were dipped in raspberry sauce.

She held the sheet tightly. Reggie crossed the large room to place the platter on the table next to the bed. His eyes darted from the tray to her, and   back to the tray. When he came closer, she heard a wheeze in his chest, and his jowls wiggled every time he turned his head. He smiled at her as he placed the tray on the table next to the bed.

"Try the tea, Miss. Pure Darjeeling." He looked around in despair at the state of the room.

"Maybe later, thank you, Reggie." She sat at the edge of the bed and smelled the rose. The sweet scent reminded her of cinnamon and cloves; it tempted her senses as well as her taste buds, making her mouth water. She put her nose into it and breathed deeply.

The casserole of bread, sausage and egg sat in a black alabaster cup, baked to a golden perfection. A finely arranged sliced orange resembled a wild flower, a porcelain teacup sat upside down on the saucer. A teapot, lemon and sugar waited on the tray's edge. It certainly was a lovely display and quite a departure from her usual breakfast of porridge and cold mead.

"You should really try the tea, Miss. Pure Darjeeling," Reggie repeated.

"Yes Reggie, you told me. Pure Darjeeling." Arose forced a laugh and a smile.

I must be dreaming. This is too perfect!

"Can I ask you a question, Reggie?" Arose asked, her mouth stuffed with oranges.

"Yes, Miss?"

"Where am I? And where is my opalescent gem?" Her anger-tainted voice held a soft growl. Nevertheless, she kept it at a slow burn, mostly because Reggie seemed to be a sweet old man and he had prepared such a lovely breakfast.

"You are on the ship the Red Spirit. Cap'm St. James carried you on board last night, with the greatest care. An' as far as your property is concerned, Miss, you have to make an appointment with the Cap'm to speak to him, directly." He hesitated for a second. "Maybe try a cup of tea. It will calm your nerves."

"Where is the Captain? I want to see him immediately." She held her nose up for emphasis.

"Oh, it's not possible, Miss. He has gone to town on personal business. We are meeting him tomorrow in the Port of San Sabastian. Will you be staying aboard?"

"The Port of San Sabastian? No! Well, that's all the way on the other side of the island. I will never be home in time. I have to go home. I must to go back to Montego Bay!" Her voice hit a high pitch as her eye caught sight of a seagull passing the window.

"Have your tea; I'll take you when you are done."
He pointed at the cup. His hand shook she stared down at
his wavering finger. At first, she wrote it off to his
advanced age but had a second to think.

She looked at the upside down teacup on the saucer.

*He really wants me to have some tea.
Hmmm...Poisoned or maybe drugged? I will have to stay
away from that.*

She turned slowly. "Yes, Reggie, I will try some."

"Cap'm says you are welcome to visit for a spell. I
expect him back after the wedding.

Arose's eyes lit up. "Wedding? Fiona's wedding?"

Reggie waved his hands in the air.

"Said too much, I did!" His skin flushed red as he
rushed out the door.

As soon as the door closed, a knock came, once
again. Arose went to the door and opened it a crack. She
spied an eye through the space.

Reggie again stood behind the door holding his
ragged hat in his hand.

Arose peered out at him, "Yes Reggie?"

"Miss? Cap'm says you are welcome to anything in
the closet."

"Thank you, Reggie." Her lips curled up at the
corners.

"You can thank the Cap'm tomorrow when you see
him."

"Yes Reggie, as soon as I receive my property back,
I will be sure to give him a proper thank you. I promise
you!"

"Miss...? Did you try the tea?"

She narrowed her eyes as her smile faded. Reggie
laughed nervously. Without a word, she slammed the door
shut.

Curiously, she reached for the porcelain cup, upside

down on a matching saucer. Her fingers grazed the bottom. Her gut told her no.

Snatching her hand away, she grabbed another slice of orange. "Let's see what the 'Cap'm' has hiding in his wardrobe." She mimicked Reggie's cockney accent.

Arose quickly opened the closet door. The smell of cedar mingled with the essence of orange on her fingertips hit her nose. "Orange and cedar," she sighed.

She pressed her nose to the door, inhaled deeply, and thought of the moment they shared in her vision. The feeling of his hand to her cheek thrilled and captivated her. She closed her eyes, her head against the door and imagined she rested on his strong shoulder. Suddenly a flash of a memory came to her. She thought of being nestled deep into the arms of the young man, Blaze, while he rode her to the safety of her uncle's ship. The only other time she had sought comfort in the arms of a stranger, amazed at herself for remembering. She hadn't thought of Blaze in years. But St. James, he would be a different story. she would never forget what he has done.

She stepped back. "Snap out of it, Rosie! He has the Gem of the Red Spirit!" She rifled through roughly fifty or more dresses, some in the newest styles directly from England and France.

"Whoa! This Cap'm' St. James is one busy man!" She pulled out a deep red satin dress, edged in gold brocade. She ran her fingers over the brocade stitches and gently touched the velvet ruffles on the skirt's edge.

It landed on the bed in a heap while she continued to dig farther into his wardrobe. She pulled out a simple beige frock with a high collar and powder blue waistcoat. Something she could be inconspicuous wearing.

She found her black pants hung over a chair and her thigh high boots, cleaned and polished, next to them. Wearing the beige dress over her skintight pants, she plunged the gleaming dagger into its sheath in her boot.

She checked to see if her gold was still in the pouch. She sighed, relieved to find it all there.

She rolled up the red dress and placed it in her satchel, throwing it over her shoulder.

He did say "Welcome to anything in the closet." She smiled at how clever she could be, how deliciously dishonest. She owed him nothing.

She walked out on deck. The sun, being on the rise, was new enough so she could look into its red center.

Already busy at work on the ship, the crewmates darted around her. One of the crew looked up and whistled. Another nudged a fellow shipmate. She shot them a look from the corner of her eye.

She found Reggie lowering the ship's dinghy into the water.

"I am ready to leave," she said loudly.

"Are ya, Miss? Already? Fast dresser. Aye? You would think a lady would want to stay on board to sample the accommodations a bit before they take their leave."

"I bet they do."

Jealousy pinched her, although she had no idea why.

"Did you try the tea?" Reggie said.

Arose thought quickly and stumbled over her words. "Yes." She smiled, hiding her lie. "Yes I did, thank you."

"Ah, you must be feeling better. Aye?" Reggie beamed. She nodded politely.

Arose stepped onto the little dinghy and Reggie carefully lowered it into the water. He climbed down and began to row toward shore.

"Reggie's water carriage at your service, Miss," he joked, beaming at her. She smiled at him, and held back the urge to give him a hug.

Reggie, being a bit older than her father, huffed at each pull of the oars. The smooth as glass water gave him no resistance. Still he stopped every now and   to catch a breath. Each time the tide would pull them out back out to sea.

Arose turned to see how much distance they had traveled. She could almost reach the bow of the ship if she had a long enough stick.

She spoke low enough for him not to hear, "At this rate we may never get to shore." She clucked her tongue and shook her head.

Reggie put his head down and puffed out his lower lip. "I'm sorry, Miss. I will get you there soon enough." He pulled the oars again, stronger and faster than before. The old man started to breathe heavily and sweat profusely.

"All right, that's enough. Come, come sit here." Carefully they switched sides.

Arose took a bottle of water and poured out some on a cloth she'd found inside a box on the dinghy. She placed it on his forehead and gave him a bit to drink.

"Not too much, Reggie. Little sips." He nodded and put his head back. She took the oars and began to row her way to shore.

"You row quite well, Miss! As good as any man I've ever seen."

"Yes, I've had some practice at being a man."

Reggie gave her a smile and closed his eyes.

They picked up speed. In moments. they were in the shoals. An angler cast his nets into deeper water, filling it full of the plentiful fish in the waters.

Arose landed the small boat on the black sand of what they called Treasure Beach. She stepped into the cool salty water. Her skirt and boots sucked up enough water to almost drag her under. The old man sat up and readied himself to jump overboard to sit under one of the thick-leaved trees that lined the beach. Her skirt soaking wet, she helped Reggie off the little boat and waved to the fisherman. "It's all right, Miss, I'm feeling a darn sight better now."

She spoke quickly to the small, frail man. "My friend here must get some rest." She pulled up her dress, dug around in her pouch, and pulled out a gold half-crown.

"Make sure he stays in the shade and drinks some water. He is the steward to Captain St. James. Take him back to the Red Spirit when he is feeling better." She handed the half-crown to the fisherman who bowed several times and repeated "*Si, si*," every few seconds.

Arose took off down the beach looking for the easiest way back inland. She ought to be home before the wedding started but it would be at least a three-hour walk back through town.

From behind her, she heard the clop, clop, clop, of a slow moving horse. She turned to see a golden horse with a bright orange mane following her down the beach.

The horse gave her a gentle nod. She approached carefully as to not scare him away. She ran her hand down its long mane, its golden coat shimmering. She felt a strong connection to the animal, and her heart skipped for a moment.

Arose looked into its large brown globe-like eye, a puff of swirling orange smoke swelled from inside. It grew until its billows filled the glassy eye, the spirit, loose from its opalescent gem home, danced around inside. Arose smiled widely and a laugh bubbled up from her throat. Inexplicably the spirit came to her in time to help. She pressed her lips to the horse's cheek and jumped on its bare back. The horse started with a quick trot. Water splashed high in the air as the pace quickened to full stride. Steam rose behind them as hot hooves hit the cool ocean water. Her hair flew in the whizzing wind. They were moving so quickly the trees were a blur.

The horse stopped at the top of the hill overlooking her home. The house held an ominous silence. The valley, covered in full-grown sugar cane stalks, would muffle her steps. A sea of green grassy fronds stretched out for miles.

A quick descent into the tall stalks would more than hide her approach to the house.

"I will be off on foot from here," she said to the horse as she dismounted. The horse turned and walked to the field and began to eat grass. She looked back; the glistening coat and mane were gone.

She disappeared into the cane field.

Chapter Ten
La Bruja

𝒟otted in small white orange blossoms, the arched doorway of Le Masion Du Mouchelle looked out of place with the swirling, foreboding air that surrounded it.

Deep green ivy and white bows wrapped each columns on either side of the door. Baskets of white flowers sat on each one of the twenty-five steps leading to the doorway, where Fiona would exit the house. Being just after dawn, she wondered who had the gumption to be up at first cock's crow to tend to these tasks. Usually it fell on her to set up the decorations for parties, prepare the dinner and organize the help. It surprised her they took care of all this without her.

As she got closer to the bottom of the great steps, she looked up to the house. She blinked at the early morning sun in her eyes. She could not make out the large brass knocker that centered each of the double doors. She stood on her toes to look in through the doorway. Despite the festive trappings, an ominous blackness covered the opening. She could see neither the door nor inside the house. She stood there for a moment and turned away, running to the rear entrance.

She turned the corner to the kitchen door. It always had an inviting charm to it. Pink and lavender flowers dripped over the planters attached to the windows. Rosemary, thyme and basil grew almost wild in a small garden next to the forest green door. The smell of baking bread and cinnamon cider wafted through the window. Arose smiled, took a cleansing breath standing at the half door. The top portion opened so she had a clear view inside the kitchen. The bottom half was latched, to keep the geese and farm animals from getting a snack within.

"Menga?" Arose called to her nanny but she did not answer. Usually, Domenga would be tending the oven, especially if she had hot cross buns baking and cider brewing. She opened the wooden door. Despite the serene scene, her heart raced. The cold, ominous air made her shiver. She looked down at chipped paint of the wooden floor before her. She stared at the pockets of missing green paint on the floor. Patterns formed faces from the missing paint. They morphed and stared back up at her. Some with mouth's open in an unheard scream, frozen, until stepping on them scratched off more paint, causing them more torment.

She shook herself out of it and walked across the room.

The only other person who would be up this early would be Libby, Menga's daughter and mother to her favorite music student, little Jessup.

"Libby?" Arose stood pensive before the doorway to the dining room. The table set for breakfast sat empty, and the house was still with a tomblike feeling.

"Hmm… where is everyone?"

Arose turned to look out the kitchen window and jumped. There by the open window Lady Katherine sat at the table. The white eyelet curtain slapped at her face as it blew in the breeze. She sat perfectly still on a hard wooden chair, staring blankly at the blotchy green painted floor.

Arose stepped over to her and squatted down to be in her line of sight. She touched Lady Katherine's hand gently, trying to rouse her from her stupor. Her ice-cold hand, usually busy with needlepoint, sat limply on her lap. She took it between hers and rubbed it briskly.

"Mother?" She waited to see if she would snap out of her trance. "Lady Katherine? Can you hear me?" Arose stood and closed the window.

She had either not slept through the night or awoken extremely early. Puffy circles under her eyes and a sallow complexion made her look ill or in desperate need of some rest.

"Mother?" She shook her shoulder. "Have you slept?"

Lady Katherine looked at Arose with a blank expression. "There is a constant buzzing in my ears that is driving me to distraction," she finally answered.

Arose held her stepmother's hand and chose her words carefully. "Mother, about Fiona's wedding. Do you think that maybe she and Mr. Ambrielle should wait a while before they marry? Maybe, an extended engagement, so they can get better acquainted."

Suddenly Lady Katherine became quite alive, as a marionette would when the puppeteer pulls its strings. "It has not even entered my mind, Arose. Anne told me what you said last night before you came out half-dressed for dinner. I have to say, this is a very sad excuse for trying to keep your sister from her happiness and the plantation under your control." Her stepmother scoffed. "Premonitions, you say. How ridiculous, your imagination is as big now as when you were a child!"

Arose backed away. "That's not the reason, Mother. We don't really know him, who is he, where did he come from?"

Suddenly pain shot from Arose's womb. She bent forward. Once again, the talisman attacked her. And Arose, without the opalescent gem's protection.

Her mother winced and placed her hands over her ears. "The buzzing! It's growing louder! I can barely hear you!"

She held her hands against her head and ran from the room, leaving Arose doubled up in pain. The smells she found so comforting before now nauseated her. Her skin itched as if spiders crawled up her legs. She pulled up her skirt and scratched until her skin was raw. The pain and nausea increased. She had to escape. She ran out of the door to the creek that passed behind the house. Coughing and sputtering, she threw up the breakfast she had aboard the ship.

After being sick, Arose trudged her way to the sugar mill. The wooden door was closed and bolted with a large lock and her without a key. She walked around back and slid the wood plank from a small window. She shimmied, head first, in through the small opening. Used to being agile with the help of the Gem of the Red Spirit, she assumed her fall to the ground would be graceful. She fell to the floor with a thud, landing on her backside. She stood and flipped her hair back, catching sight of the open window in front of her.

Unwittingly she stood before the opening, facing the rear of her family home. There stood Ambrielle, standing at the door, glaring through the window at her. The dirty feeling was back. His indecorous stare haunted her wherever she went. Arose ducked down and slid out of view.

Thinking she would be out of his line of sight, she inhaled a cleansing breath. In place of the usual scent of hibiscus and ocean breezes, the pungent smell of death filled the air.

She pinched her nose and checked around the floor for a dead rat or armadillo, which may have slunk inside and died. Searching, pitchfork in hand, she hoped to unearth the victim, maybe give it a proper burial or at least stop it from smelling up the room. Sniffing, she went hunting for the source of the smell. Behind the stone chimney, a tall closet for pokes and brooms hid in a small space. The overpowering stench made her stomach turn, tasting the vomit while she opened the door. Looking down, she half expected to find something curled up dead on the floor. A thick black sticky mess soaked into the dirt where a broom handle met the ground. Her eyes adjusted to the darkness and followed the branch up until she stared into a pair of opaque eyes.

She jumped back three steps and slammed into the wooden wall. In front of her, a goat's head, impaled on a broomstick, stared out at her with white eyes. Around the goat's horns hung one of the hens, its neck broken. Blood, dripping down the goat's snout.

"*Brujeria*! Witchcraft!" She hissed and slammed the door.

Morel's powers were strong, but maybe she could weaken them. She stoked the fire in the boiler. When it reached a furious glow, she took the dead animals and threw them into the heated kiln. She closed the door and watched from behind the grate while the dead animals burned. Black blood bubbled while they seared in the furnace. Sparks flew off the goat's horns and bounced against the walls of the incinerator as if they were alive. Meanwhile screeching hisses came from inside, anguished voices begging to escape the chamber. She covered her ears to mute the sound, her hands shaking, the pleading voices becoming too much for her.

The horrible shrieks faded. She heard the coo of a morning dove, and realized there had been a constant whirring in her ears, which had stopped. Previously imperceptible, it had been there for some time. As in noises only heard after they have ended, like chattering of the crowd at a ball that suddenly fall silent when a glass breaks.

"Morel has been weakened." She had a thought. She closed her eyes.

"*Bessonth? Can you hear me?*"

Bessonth's voice came clear in her mind.

"*Yes chil'.*"

"*I have burned a Voodoo altar in the work shed. Can you escape now?*"

"*I cannot leave here.*"

"Why Bess, what happened?"

"I will be free soon, when de time be right. I will escape my captors."

"I need you right now I have to cleanse this space of Morel's voodoo spell. Tell me what to do."

"The herbs chil', do you still have dem?"

Bess had many herbs growing in her cart in the bog. She always made sachets for Arose, filled with lavender, sage and rosemary. Arose ran to her leather satchel and pulled out a sachet pillow Bess had made long ago.

"Yes! Now what?"

"Find a blue bottle, fill it with pure water, add a handful of sand, and the herbs. A powerful wash this will be."

She put the sachet to her nose. The dried herbs inside were still fragrant. On a shelf, she found a large blue bottle. She ripped open the sachet and filled the bottle with its contents. She ran to the sand pile, and put in a handful of sand,   filled the bottle with water.

"You must chant and cleanse the area. I will tell you what to say."

Arose circled the area three times and said:

Nan dlo ak zèb rafine rete isit le pou mwen li ye.
Purification Et netwaye être magique plas sa a.
Manman vant ba ou benediksyon pou rite sa a
Ban m 'pouvwa a al goumen fòs sa ki mal la
(Pure water and herbs refined, clean this place.)
(Cleansed and protected be this magical space.)
(Mother Earth give your blessing to this rite.)
(Give me the power to fight the evil's might.)

She poured the water out onto the ground where the sticky mess remained. The blood bubbled up from the earth. It was black at first but turned as white as sea foam.

Arose saved the last drops and cleansed the poisonous blood from her hands.

Through with the incantation and cleansing, she gathered her things. She tore off the blood-covered dress and threw it into the kiln. Being the third week of June, the stifling mill smoldered with the growing embers of the animal's remains. Sweating profusely, she sought a way to cool down. She cut the legs from her breeches and slid them on. The extremely short black breeches revealed her long tanned legs.

A long sword sat in a corner of the room. She picked it up and sliced the air. A makeshift dummy hung from a low beam; a smile curved her lip as she cleaved it through. The thrust would have been an instant kill. Picking a coal out of the dead kiln, she wrote "CAP'M ST. JAMES" across its chest. She gave it an angry shove. It swung to and fro like a corpse on the business end of a hangman's noose.

She wrapped her knuckles in burlap and balled up her fists. Her strikes at the heavy bag stuffed with straw, thumped in triplicate. Relief tumbled over her and she cracked her stiff neck, bouncing lightly on her toes. She planted her feet to add more power to her punches. Her next round landed square, punctuated with a high kick, hard enough to knock the effigy's head clean off, if it had one. She limped away on a sore leg.

The room became hot and steamy while the noon sun beat down on the tin roof of the sugar mill. The time of the wedding was nearing. Guests would be arriving soon. The mid-morning Caribbean heat blasted Arose the moment Lady Katherine pulled back the large wooden doors.

Her stepmother stood motionless in the doorway, but Arose did not stop swinging the sharp blade, to greet her.

Lady Katherine spoke toward the sound of steel

whistling through the air, still oblivious to all the evil circling around her. Still, she held a commanding presence.

"You should be ready to greet your sister's guests by now, Nessarose." Using Arose's given name made her seethe.

Arose straightened up from her crouched fighting stance and squinted into the blaze of light; seeing only a curved silhouette.

Arose's long, tousled hair hung over her eyes, sweat dripped down her nose. She thrust out her left hip and placed her curled fingers on it; her other hand held the sword's hilt.

"They are her guests, for her wedding, let her greet them."

Her mother expertly lifted an arched eyebrow; the subtle gesture spoke a thousand words. "Your sister is in her room, prostrate before her wedding. We can't have her running around in the heat greeting guests."

Arose rolled her eyes and changed the subject.

"Mother, did Fiona receive a gift with the marriage proposal?"

"Yes, she did. Mary Murphy, Harold's closest relative, sent a gift with her brother. The pewter pitcher surrounded by laurel on the dining table last night. Lovely, isn't it?"

"Um mm." *The pewter pitcher.*

Her mother looked down. "Too bad Mary Murphy has already sent a note that she will not be able to attend the wedding today. Luckily she is sending her sons in her stead."

"Her sons?" Her eyes rolled around her head. Shaw Murphy and his ill-mannered brothers terrorizing the wedding guests would not be welcome and she would have to watch her every step to be sure not to cross their path.

"Mother, do you still have that ringing in your ears?"

"What ringing? I have no clue to what you talking about. Prepare yourself for the wedding. I have put a dress out for you."

"Yes, the party." She would have to put the situation out of her head for now and not say a word of what she learned. What had transpired had to be a secret, Bessonth waited underground and her life depended on it. At the party, she would meet Captain St. James and retrieve her opalescent gem. After which Bessonth could break free.

She grabbed the leather satchel holding the red dress and slung it across her back. She passed through the wooden doors into the baking sun, in her short black breeches and boots. Her shirt, tied under her breasts, clung damply to her body with sweat from the furnace. The sun burned her face as she turned to look down the road to see if, maybe, St. James would just happen to ride over the hill.

Arose looked over the beige rocky ground to where sky met earth. The horizon blurred as heat vapors rose up. Patches of gold reeds poked through the sandy soil as a hot mid-day breeze blew her blonde streaked hair from her sweaty face.

From the middle of the road, she glanced back at the sugar mill. There stood Harold Ambrielle in the doorway. He looked quite odd in an ill-fitting wedding jacket and trousers. She hissed at him like a feral cat.

His expression made her skin crawl like worms on rotted flesh. His eyes fixed on her, a combination of lust and disgust on his face.

She read his thoughts. His thighs were between her legs as his hands were around her throat. He thrust inside her as he twisted her neck while she gasped for air. She shut the image out of her mind.

Chapter Eleven
A Cask Of Rum

Arose stood frozen in the middle of the road before the house. Harold leered at her from the doorway of the mill, evil thoughts permeating his mind. Her legs trembled beneath her; she looked down to the ground, the small pebbles at her feet bounced along the surface. The entire ground under her shook.

The road spread out before her. From where she stood, a long length of golden dirt rose uphill into the horizon. She looked up to the top of the hill. Dust filled the hot June air from the dry earth road. Her sharp eye caught sight of something beyond the top of the hill ebbing out and into her line of sight. Finally, two figures popped up over the crest.

The hoofbeats grew louder and faster. As they closed in, she saw neither rider noticed her. Neither slowed, nor banked their horses right or left. Arose dashed across the road and tumbled into the bushes lining the picket fence to the house.

The horses sped past her, the two carefree men astride their mounts engaged in riotous laughter.

Dust and rocks flew in the dense air, hanging there indefinitely, creating an opaque cloud. The riders continued down the road. Arose ran blindly toward the house to get out of the deluge of yellow dirt that clung to the glistening sweat of her body.

Running up the steps, she found the door and entered. Coughing to clear her lungs, she slammed the door behind her.

Down the hall, her sisters, Anne and Fiona, burst

out of their room and appeared before her.

"What on earth happened to you?" asked Fiona, who wore a white crocheted dress. Anne giggled, watching over Fiona's shoulder.

"Some fools nearly ran me over in the road. They kicked up so much dirt I could barely see." Arose entered her room where a bathtub waited, the water, cold and murky from the soap used during her sister's baths. She hated using the same bath water and called for Libby.

A servant, not much older than she came, in and looked into the bath, "You be wanting some fresh water I suppose?"

"Yes please, Libby, if it would not be too much trouble," Arose asked with a sigh. Libby walked out of the room heading for the back door.

"Hmm," Anne said, "She wouldn't refill the tub for me!"

Arose grinned. "Well, you never say please."

"I don't have to." Anne held her nose up. "There is no reason to be polite to a slave."

"She is not a slave!" Arose's ire rising. "You best be more polite around me!"

Anne's eyes opened wide and her mouth remained open, but no words came out.

Her sisters nudged each other, watching while she stepped behind the dressing screen and tossed her clothes over the top.

"So... there were fools in the road? Whomever are you talking about?" Fiona said, lifting her chin to project her voice over the partition.

Anne whispered to Fiona, "It must have been Captain St. James. Libby said he just arrived."

Arose, hearing, quickly poked her head out from behind the silk enclosure and seethed. Her eyes narrowed. "St. James," she growled, the name alone infuriating her.

Anne stepped back, surprised at Arose's reaction.

"But-but there are many guests coming in now," Anne stammered. They ran to the window facing the open garden and stared out through the lace curtain. Sprinkled with white parasols, the green lawn sparkled like diamonds in the sun. Women with high-collared pale dresses and men in red velvet coats dabbed the sweat from their brows.

Fiona sniffed the air, crinkled her nose; she looked over to Arose, her skin blotchy and dirt-stained.

"Rosie! You are a mess, and you reek! You should be dressed by now. Step to the tub and wash off that dirt. I can't wait to be Missus Harold Ambrielle."

"Trust me, you could," Arose said under her breath.

"Why? What do you mean, Rosie?" Fiona asked innocently.

"She meant nothing, didn't you Arose? You meant nothing by that." Anne shot back at Arose, silencing her with a scowl.

Arose, not being the kind to save her sister's feelings for the sake of the truth, blurted out, "You should run, Fiona. He is not who you think he is!"

Anne shouted, "You are wrong, I won't let you fill Fiona's head with your jealous ravings. Go, go," Anne whispered to Fiona, pushing her out of the room. Anne quietly closed the door, the pair giggling as they returned to their room.

Arose slid wearily into the lukewarm bathwater. It turned the same dusty color as the road below her window.

She soaped herself slowly, the natural sponge scrubbing the last remnants of dirt into the bubbly water. She relaxed into the tub, feeling her tensions slip away. She felt herself sliding down into the tub but the ache in her pelvis returned. She tried to look around the room but she could not turn her head left or right. Not able to lift herself, she slid, helpless, under the surface, water passing her lips, directly under her nose. Her eyes widened as she tried with all her might to rise out of the tub.

Alone in the room but feeling hands squeezing her shoulders and pushing her down, she let out a high-pitched whine, when she finally succumbed to the force on her.

She held her breath and went under the surface; only her wide eyes were above a soapy bath. She tried desperately to hang onto the rim of the tub, when she lost her grip, her nails squeaked as they ran down into the bath water.

The back of her head thumped at the tub's bottom, her hair swelled with water and floated up around her face.

Libby came into the room, a shining pewter pitcher in her hands.

The talisman!

"Libby! Don't use that!" Her stepmother ran to the chambermaid and whisked it out of her hands.

"This is Fiona's wedding gift from her new sister." Her mother quickly walked out of the house toward the great lawn.

The weight on Arose's shoulders eased, and the paralysis keeping her from moving disappeared. She shot up from the water and took a big breath of air.

She jumped out of the bath and wrapped a soft gauzy sheet around her soaked body. She left puddles as she walked to the window and pulled back the lace curtain, watching her mother cross the great lawn with the powerful article.

Lady Katherine poured out the pitcher into the rose garden. The green stems had turned black and the white petals browned, curling into themselves. They disintegrated into the sandy dirt.

Spritely bouncing behind her mother, the familiar orange wisp of the Red Spirit danced along, unseen by all but her. She smiled. She caught sight of a young man outside her window, sitting atop a large stallion.

She concealed herself behind the wall and spied on him from the lace and damask curtain. An older rider rode up seconds later.

The younger man's horse reared up on its hind legs. The rider settled him gently to the ground and bounded off his mount in a smooth clean motion. Light brown hair brushed his shoulders, clear blue eyes danced under its strands. The mustache and beard encircled a warm smile, the clef in his chin perceptible under the scruff that lined his sturdy jaw. He reached for the reins of his companion's horse.

The other rider dismounted carefully. His dark piercing eyes swept the surroundings from under his wide-brimmed hat. He fingered the jewel-encrusted dagger at his waist as if daring someone to leap out of the shadows.

Edmund said, "Do you remember this house, Blaze?"

"Yes, sir, it hasn't changed much."

"Those are the two that almost ran me down on the road." Not willing to be seen, she hid behind the lace. *That is Uncle Edmund and his steward Blaze. Still his servant I suppose. Anne thought it might have been St. James. Ha!* She laughed.

From her vantage point, she studied Blaze. His cream colored shirt, open midway down a tanned chest, billowed in the breeze. Muscular forearms flexed as he lifted the saddle from his stallion. Stuffed into the tops of his calf-high brown boots, the legs of his tight beige breeches showed his well-formed legs. Arose dragged her eyes over his manhood, round and large. He had a self-assured swagger, highlighted by the sway of his soft leather coat.

She smiled and bit into her lower lip.

Blaze moved smoothly from one task to another, fluid and in control of every inch of his body. Arose began to let her mind and her eyes roam over him. She wondered how the skin of his shoulders would feel on her lips. If she swept her tongue along his ear lobe, would he nuzzle her neck in return? She lingered there to watch him as he moved; she realized her nakedness only feet from him, hidden from his view by the damask and lace curtain.

She watched as he squatted to check the horse's legs and hooves. Her imagination swirled around thoughts of her between his spread knees as he looked up to her, almost feeling his hands massaging her thighs.

"Blaze," she moaned "Cap'm St. James has nothing on you." Suddenly a breeze swirled around her legs. She snatched the cloth tightly over her body and spun to face the door. Harold stood almost in the center of the room, a sickening look of lust on his greasy face.

"Get out of my room!" Arose snarled. She shoved him out through the door, slamming it in his face.

She pressed an ear to the closed door. Her sisters stepped into the hall, the bride giggled and Anne yelled, "You're not supposed to be in here! No one can see the bride before the wedding!"

Harold stomped his large feet down the hall and the front door slammed as he walked from the house.

"Demented," Arose mumbled under her breath.

A pale peach gown lay on her bed. She looked it over. The high needlelace collar would skim the bottom of her chin and the high empire waist would make her lean muscular body look short and round. She tossed it into the corner of the room.

She opened her leather satchel. The satin dress she pinched from the Red Spirit waited inside.

"Libby, come help me dress." The light-skinned black woman stepped into the room.

Her eyes opened wide when she saw the peach dress in a heap.

"Oh, you are looking for some trouble," she said in a singsong voice.

"Maybe, but that frock is just awful. It wouldn't show a bit of my best attributes." Arose smiled with a sly-fox grin.

"You keep showing those things off and you will have half the town after you." Libby warned as she tightened her corset.

"It's all right as long as it's the right half." Arose giggled and Libby snickered.

"Where did this dress come from, Miss Rosie?" Libby looked over the bodice as she brought it to her.

"Don't worry about where it came from, the less you know the better." The young woman helped her into the evening dress and buttoned it up the back. Silk buttons went from the tailbone up to the high collar, as fastened with a brocade loop.

It fit as if it were made for her, beige raw silk with gold thread trailed down a center panel in the front. The embroidery showed delicate pink roses with emerald green leaves and stems. It cut tightly around her bust line so that the beauty mark between her breasts appeared demure yet sultry. The French cuff sleeves were trimmed in the gold brocade that matched the trim of the inset. The balance of the dress was red satin, which gleamed iridescent when it caught the light. A gathered peplum made her waist appear tiny and trailed down her back. The dress followed the curve of her body like a fitted waistcoat. The layers of ruffles skimmed the floor, and a short bustle and train trailed behind her.

She tossed her hair into a mass of curls and quickly arranged some wispy strands to tumble over her shoulders.

Arose exited her room, red silk slippers in hand. Her bare feet padded softly on the marble floor. She wanted to avoid seeing anyone, including her sisters. They would send her back to her room to change into the peach frock and pull her hair back severely to match theirs. She relaxed the moment she finally made it outside the house and put her shoes on.

Uncle Edmund and her father were engaged in

conversation they both seemed to enjoy. They stood laughing under the trellis of Petit Rouge grapes. The vines were an import from their native France. The flowers were fading in the June sun and now small round wine grapes emerged. Not only did the arrangement smell fragrant, but it also provided shade from the scathing sun.

She scanned the guests for Blaze, looking for someone who would be at least a head above the crowd, with his sandy blond hair skimming his shoulders. Her heart pounded a bit, more excited than she should be to see a mere servant. She realized her purpose—it would be a necessity to stop thinking about Blaze for the moment. She must find Captain St. James. Not knowing what he looked like, she could only imagine that such a pirate would be dressed in the wide hat and cape she saw before she unfortunately went unconscious.

Still, her thoughts drifted back to the handsome Blaze. Maybe if he saw her with Edmund he would come by and join them. She smiled widely with a brave face, breezed up to her father and looped her arm under his.

"Hello, Father," she said and warmly kissed his cheek.

"Uncle Edmund! You look dashing as always." Arose curtsied, grasped her uncle's outstretched hand, and clasped it gently.

"Good day, child!" His voice boomed with strength as it carried into the breeze. "You have been missed greatly in Marmara."

"I miss being there, Uncle, but I'm happy to see you looking so well." Her affection for her uncle was genuine. She enjoyed their time together on their voyages and the secrets they shared.

"Did you see I brought your old friend Blaze to the affair?" Edmund said proudly.

"Yes, yes. I did." she said nonchalantly.

"Do you know a Captain St. James? I hear he is

going to attend." She looked around for a plumed hat and black cape.

"Err… yes, Arose, I do in fact know him." Her uncle looked at her strangely.

Uncomfortable quiet came over the small group while she looked around her attention so obviously not on the present conversation. Her father broke the silence. "Arose, get a rum for Edmund. There is not a drop on the table!"

Uncle Edmund laughed. "Yes, a man could die of thirst waiting for a drink here."

The bottles on the tables held red wine on the tables, their own family brand. Several pewter cups were strewn around, but no rum. Arose would have to return to the house to fetch the decanter for him.

"Yes, Father. I will be right back with your drink, Uncle." She returned to the house. The quiet hallway echoed her footsteps on the marble. Darkened rooms and high ceiling kept the interior air cool. She would have to pass many dark hallways before she made it to the parlor, where the rum cask rested on a large credenza.

Despite the hot June afternoon, the parlor remained cool and dark. She stood by the arched doorway to survey the room. She knew stepping in, her eyes would take a moment to adjust. Blind for the first few moments she crept in, her hands before her, leading her on. The chill of the room sent a shiver down her. The chatter from the party faded in the silence of the room, designed to be acoustically perfect.

The wood slat blinds were tied down to prevent their opening so the sunlight could not fade the red settee. Still the afternoon sun found a way in. A single beam stretched through the far end of the room, to touch the back wall. Treading carefully on the polished wood floor so as not to slip or make noise, she became more at ease, her eyes finally able to make out shapes and colors. Anne and

Fiona's needleworks decorated the far corner. A flute and pianoforte were set with the sheet music laid open to the pieces they had worked on in preparation of the day's festivities. The chairs and couches were pushed against the wall in case anyone cared to dance after dinner.

Arose located the small cask of rum on a wooden cart with large wheels. She chose the decanter embossed with a tall ship, a good choice for a seafaring man.

While she poured, the amber liquid spilled over her fingers. She licked the droplets.

A deep voice came from the entrance. "Watch out there, you may get yourself drunk and lose your inhibitions."

She gasped, caught off guard by the presence in the room. She didn't know the voice.

Her thoughts went immediately to Blaze. She spoke without turning. "I'll have you know I have very few inhibitions." She spun, expecting to see Blaze, revealing a flirtatious smile.

Her eyes opened wide and her stomach turned. Harold Ambrielle stood in the arched doorway of the room.

"YOU!"

Arose's mind went back to her visions. The first when she met him in the dining room, the other while she lingered in the road. He frightened her, but she held a brave face.

"Never mind about my inhibitions, and I would appreciate if you didn't follow me around." She took the filled decanter and headed toward the door.

"We are very much alike, you and I. I saw you spying out the window. You're no better than me."

Arose's stomach lurched. She tasted bile in her mouth.

"But I'm not a big pig," she spat back, hoping her words would sear him.

She felt brave enough to pass him. Never would he

dare to touch her in her own home, minutes before his wedding. He grabbed her by the arm and pulled her into the room. The decanter fell from her hand, the rum spilling onto the wood floor. She could hear the bottle glugging, emptying its contents. He stepped further into the shadows, dragging her with him.

Circumstances aside, she knew it would be not likely he would let the insult of calling him a pig go but she was unprepared for his untamed rage. Taking her by the upper arms, he shook her, his hands feeling like meat hooks on her. Her whole body jerked about like a rag doll. She felt as through her head would snap off her from her neck and shoulders. She tugged her arms away, breaking his hold on her. Not willing to give in to his brutality, she slapped him hard on his cheek, her hand exploding in pain. Her palm's imprint plastered from his ear to the corner of his mouth. Red came from a cut that opened on his lip.

He twisted his face up into a perverted smile. Touching the blood on his lip, he looked down at his fingers, then back at her, black eyes seared her from under a furrowed brow.

"I knew you would like it rough," he hissed out in a moan. Before she could brace herself, Harold connected the back of his hand to the underside of her jaw, sending her back a few steps. Pain burst in her chest when she slammed against the wall. She felt herself fading out of consciousness. Plaster crumbled down her arms, plinking as it hit the floor. In her stupor, she imagined raindrops tickling her skin and crackling on a tin roof.

Despite the pain and deliria, all she could think of how slight her sister was; she hoped she would see a better side of him. He would break her as easily as a china teacup.

She managed to shake off the fading feeling, yet unable to move, her arms hung limp at her sides, her knees buckled under her she and she slid down the wall. Lifting her from under her arms, he made sure to crush any armor left between him and her virtue. Air expressed from her lungs as he kept her upright by using his body to pin her against the wall. She tried to muster the strength to scream but before she let out the smallest yelp, he clamped his hand over her mouth. Her eyes were wide she searched the area for a weapon.

She felt his hardness grow while he rubbed his manhood against her leg. He moaned and with a breathy whisper said, "You like that, yea, yea, I know you do."

He grasped her throat and squeezed, the pain from her neck becoming unbearable. His heavy breathing into her face caused her to smell his rotten breath, his teeth covered in a yellow slime. He finally released her aching jaw.

"Where is it? Where is the opalescent gem?" his voice scratched, almost the same as the boar's grunts. She looked up into his face, her eyes wide open. His flat nose dripped in slimy wetness while tusks emerged from the sides of his mouth.

"I don't know!" she lied. "I passed out; when I woke, it was gone. I don't know who took it." She surprised herself when the words slipped out of her mouth. Why would she want to protect St. James? She could have set Ambrielle on his trail. She owed him nothing.

He moved his hand down to her leg and grabbed a hold of her skirt, lifting it to her thigh.

"If I can't have that right now, I will take what I want." He passed his hand over the supple skin of her inner thigh. "Is this a virgin twat like your sister's? Or have you been greased before?"

She tightened the muscles of her legs, squeezing them together. His fingers fought the vice grip she held over her virginity. Arose challenged him to look her straight in the eye. He averted his gaze down, staring instead at her throbbing breasts.

A hand appeared on Harold's shoulder. It clamped

down and pulled Harold off his feet, tossing him back several steps. Relief cascaded over her. Able to move, Arose bent over, coughing to catch her breath. She lifted her eyes to see Blaze in the sunbeam that escaped the shutters. Her heart thumped in her chest; she wanted to crawl into the nearest corner and hide leap into his arms at the same time. A bright smile illuminated his face while he clenched his fists at his sides, the muscles in his neck straining.

Harold's face changed back to human. Letting out a jittery laugh, he backed toward the door.

"No, no. I am… assessing my property in the house when the young lady came into the room," he drawled.

"I am not your property, and neither is anything in this house!" Arose snapped back, holding her aching neck.

"It's not going to be for very much longer. Lady Katherine saw to that. You are not the only heir now." As if this venom was not strong enough to harm her, he kept going, "That bitch that bore you is dead. And being she was only a shade darker than you, maybe you will be my property now," his glee was palpable. The thought of tearing her down thrilled him.

Arose felt her nails, she only wished they were sharp enough to slice into him. She lunged for his face. Blaze caught her in mid-air, his hands around her waist and held her aloft, not allowing her feet to reach the ground.

"Haven't you had enough for one day?" he said, holding her close.

Harold laughed and marched from the room wiping the blood pooling on his chin. He slammed the front door.

Blaze put her down and stood close, eyeing her every move. He waited for a few tense moments to pass. "Are you all right, Miss?" he finally asked.

Arose still felt the nauseating pressure of Harold's body against hers.

"I guess I should be thanking you," she said,

finding the words.

"Who is that jester?" he asked. "I will tell the host to remove him from the grounds."

"It won't help." She looked up at him "He is the groom." She shrugged.

She stepped into the rum. The carpet squished under her feet; a   towel hung from the rolling bar. Pulling it off, she used it to blot the stain from the carpet. Her hands still shook from the encounter.

"Would you mind staying with me while I refill this bottle?" She picked up the decanter and brought it back to the cart. She tried not to raise her eyes to meet his.

"Don't worry, Miss, I will take care of Edmund. I do it all the time." He gently took the vessel out of her hand, filled it and closed it with a stopper.

"I remember you. You are Blaze, my uncle's squire."

"I was," he said with a smile.

"You are my pirate friend. We played together on board the ship."

"Arose, yes, I know." He searched her eyes. He opened his mouth to speak but Arose jumped up as if something grabbed her.

St. James! I must find Captain St. James! Her mind was racing, aware of the fleeting time.

"Wait, wait, wait. Belay that thought. I need to find someone right away." Arose lifted her skirt and ran to the door.

Blaze mouthed the word back, "Belay?" and then smiled. "Aye, aye Cap'm," he joked.

She poked her head back in. "You will take that rum to my uncle, won't you?" She smiled her most impish grin.

"Yes, Miss" he answered obediently. "Oh, and you look lovely in the red dress."

Arose took off toward the great lawn.

"Thank you!" she called back without stopping, waving her hand in the air.

St. James! I need to find St. James and the opalescent gem!

Chapter Twelve
The Hunt For St. James

The train of the red dress trailed behind her as she turned the corner to the exit. Standing on the front terrace, she looked back through the door into the darkness of the den.

She turned her back when Blaze walked out of the room and down the hall to the kitchen at the back of the house. She promised herself she would thank him properly.

Blaze had the gait of a man of power and sureness, attributes not usually found in a servant. Her uncle must have given him much latitude to build such confidence. Arose found that incredibly attractive in itself but he remained so beneath her station. Arose couldn't see herself falling in love with him. She saw herself using him, abusing him, and throwing him aside, possibly hurting a dear man in the meantime.

She required a man who would stir her passions, someone she could trade barbs with, be angry at, fall into bed, and rip each other apart while making passionate love. She wanted someone who could match the tigress in her soul.

She wanted St. James.

Still, Arose watched all the exits from where he could emerge. Her eyes darted from the crowd, where she searched for St. James, to the back door, waiting for Blaze leave the house. It didn't take long for her wait to be over. The light green door flew open, taken by the tropical breeze. Through the kitchen door strode Blaze. His confident swagger drew eyes and he strode across the deep green grass. The beige kid leather long coat fluttered with each step.

Blaze approached Edmund with a smile, his arms outstretched holding the prized decanter of rum in one hand and two cut crystal glasses in the other. Quite pleased, Edmund took the fine crystal and held it to the light. He slapped Blaze on the back with a hearty, "Good man!"

Still his steward. She shook her head and clucked her tongue. *He really could have been so much more. He is smart, handsome, a great sailor and a leader. He has a refined stature not many have, especially after spending so much time a servant. In another life, given the right schooling and opportunities he would be master and commander of his own ship.* Watching Blaze move around the crowd, he reminded her of a dancer. He wooed each lady by his presence. She tried to catch a glimpse of his aura but without Gem of the Red Spirit, that power, like so many others, disappeared with any hope. Blind in her third eye, she felt uneasy.

From her perch on the front terrace, she looked away and continued her search for St. James somewhere on the Great Lawn. On the terrace, the black slate covering the area crackled under her feet. Pacing and wringing her hands were a sure sign that her nerves were jangled, and it showed on her face.

Blaze was able to see over the crowd, being a head taller than most of the guests littering the lawn. He worried the altercation with the brute had hurt her. She seemed nervous, and with good reason. He did not know many women who, after dealing with such a horror, could maintain their composure. He stared at her profile. The curve of her cheek had not changed in the ten years since he left her on the dock at Marmara. The swelling that should have been evident on her jaw already receded, the clef on her chin apparent. The curls, which had come loose from her sun-touched chignon, played on her shoulders. The man in the den thought of her as a possession. To him she could be none other than an angel, a brave solitary angel who needed his protection.

Arose, feeling his eyes heavy on her, cast a glance in his direction, when their eyes met, she turned her head. He smiled and watched her lip curl from the side of her face. His eyes gleamed while a rosy glow spread over her. It warmed him but her eyes were frightened. The same protective urges aroused with in him, along with something new, a want and a need to hold her in his arms, to lay her in the grass and make love to her.

Spotting three pewter cups on the table next to him, he picked them up one by one, threw them into the air; as he caught one, he would toss it up again. The cups cascaded from hand to hand in perfect time. He focused on the rhythm and balance of his practiced trick. A crowd began to form around him. The onlookers around him pitched him their emptied vessels. Each time adding another and another, the ladies and gentlemen surrounding him broke out into applause.

Catching the six cups in his arms, he smiled and bowed in her direction. She applauded by lightly clapping her fingers together, a sassy ovation. Her face with a gleaming smile showed some relief. His hair swept his broad shoulders as he spun to bow to his fans.

When he turned back, she wasn't on the deck. He walked over to Edmund and put the cups on his table. Resting in a thatch back chair Edmund said, "Nice show, me boy. Keep that up and the ladies won't let you back to your ship."

Blaze looked down at his rope worn hands, "There is only one person I did that for. But what of it, Edmund? She seems to want nothing of me now," he said, his voice halfhearted.

Edmund laughed, "Who can blame her? Look at yer ugly mug."

Blaze's crystal blue eyes smiled first, before his handsome face burst into laughter.

"No," he said, getting grave a second later. "I'm afraid there is something dreadful going on here."

"Well, just keep your eye on her, keep her safe," said Edmund between sips of his rum. Blaze sighed with relief when he finally spotted Arose sauntering through the crowd, her bosom high and proud. Blaze whispered, "Done and done." He watched her pass, his eyes over the rim of his cup. He held it up to his lips. Arose turned. He caught her eye, but this time he held her stare and winked.

Tingling shot down her legs. She had to squelch an impulse to run and jump up into his arms, begging for his love and protection. Feeling, once again, the girl-like crush, she remembered from long ago, although now, she wanted something more.

Perhaps they would start with a kiss on the hand during their chat and end with him burying his...

Rosie! You are doing it again... you have to find St. James!

She looked away, hoping he hadn't seen the need in her eyes. How could she enjoy herself while Bessonth remained in such serious danger—the guilt would not allow her. She had to get the Gem of the Red Spirit back; she had to find St. James.

Theirs being one of the wealthiest homes on the island, gossip, as usual, abounded about around town. Word about one of the Du Mouchelle girls receiving a marriage proposal spread like wildfire through Montego Bay. People came from all around to join the festivities. Intent on finding the illusive captain, she had to sift through many men. Descending the steps, she breezed through some guests milling about. Young men chatting stopped to give her a bow. She made sure to hear each young man's name.

The list of introductions went on:

"Miss Du Mouchelle, I am pleased to introduce you to Charles Ambrose."

"Come meet Mr. Lawrence Powell."

"Miss Nessarose, please allow me to introduce the new Deacon of St. James Parish, David DeBrun." Men smiled and bowed, while staring directly at her bosom, and then began whispering amongst themselves when she drifted off to the next group.

On the great lawn, long tables sat in the shade of wide umbrellas. The main dais, draped in flowers, sat closer to the house in the shade of the grape arbor. She made her way around the makeshift arch and shuddered. What would be the outcome of her sister's union with this man? If she could find St. James in time to return the Gem of the Red Spirit to her, she could stop the wedding. And if he refused…

She spotted Shaw Murphy standing in the shadow house. His brothers were making a game out of tossing pebbles into the crowd of pleasantly chatting guests. Leery that they would recognize her, she stood behind a thick row of hedges and watched them.

Shaw's blackened eyes were almost closed shut; his bulging nose was blood red and swollen. The brothers stood by themselves, away from the other guests. She ducked around them.

Arose folded her arms and surveyed the grounds, watching for St. James. Once again, she climbed to the patio to see a better view. Standing like a constable at his post, she surveyed the area. Her eye caught the spry movement of a feather on a plumed hat. The man, wearing a velvet cape, chased a woman into the sugar cane.

"St. James!" she growled.

They laughed and ran in circles around a kapok tree, she dodging every attempt he made to hold her in his arms. Jealousy welled up, over whelming her. How could she be so wrong about such a seducer? In her vision, he reached out to touch her as if they were one already, but in reality, he chased down the first skirt he saw.

She dashed down the stairs. Sure, she had finally found her prey. The tigress in her took over and she followed her animal instincts in the brush.

Arose ran after them into the sugar cane field where they entered, following their tracks through soft fertile earth. The thickly plumbed hat hung over a stalk of cane whipping in the breeze. She crept up slowly. In the distance, she heard gentle moans and smacking lips, she rolled her eyes up into her head.

A high voice giggled. Arose heard the rustling of the sugar stalks; undoubtedly, the rogue was busily crushing down the cane to make a bed for him and his newest conquest. Just then, a shirt came flying over her head and hung precariously from the tops of the canes. The moans became louder and more intense while she moved closer to St. James and the woman.

Finally, she found the two on top of crushed cane, moving rhythmically. Kisses and moans so loud the entire party must have heard them, if not for the chatter and music. The girl's opaque white stockings rolled down exposing her thighs and calves; her leather boots dug into the back of his legs. He knelt before her, cupping her rear to hold her hips high. She passed her hands over his bare chest, moaning, as she grew closer to her climax.

Arose smirked. In the middle of their tryst, she would jump out and demand he give her back the Gem of the Red Spirit, and he would not deny her.

The girl's pitch grew higher, St. James bringing her to orgasm.

"Slut! *Kochon!*" Arose jealously whispered, watched for another moment. St. James started to breathe more heavily. This would be her chance. She wanted to catch him in the act, to brand him a thief and gigolo. But time was waning, she needed the opalescent gem and she needed it now to save Bessonth and her family.

Arose leapt out into the clearing, "ST. JAMES!" she yelled, pointing down.

The man stopped his thrusts and looked up at Arose. "No, dear girl, I am not St. James."

Arose winced and her face blushed profusely. "Uncle Edmund!" His partner opened her eyes, and covered her face with her dark hands. Arose stifled a gasp, holding up her hand to block the sight.

"Libby? Oh, I'm sorry," she whispered but the words caught in her throat.

She turned and ran back through the cane. Her head swimming, she made a wrong turn and got lost in the field. When she found her way out, she walked through the crowd, avoiding all eyes. By the time Arose returned from her chase, the ceremony had already taken place and the 'I do's' were said.

She had failed to find St. James and stop the wedding. Now, she would resume the hunt for St. James and find the Gem of the Red Spirit. Afterward, she could carry on with her plan to save Bessonth and somehow in the meantime help her family.

Ambrielle stood, smiling greedily and eagerly collecting whatever wedding gifts the guests brought, he did not look anywhere except in a little black book, the feather tip of his quill twitching as if it were alive.

The sun set over the lush hilly sugar cane plantation. Shades of blue, orange and pink gleamed on the horizon. With everyone duly consumed in the festivities, she flitted from group to group, waiting for someone to introduce her. She waited to meet every man there but finding St. James not among them, she excused herself and went on to the next group.

Arose felt many eyes on her, but above them all she felt Blaze. The weight of his stare electrified her. She could almost feel his hand around her waist and his lips on her neck; she strove to keep her concentration. She caught his eye; she turned to smile wishing she could forget her troubles and join his party. He stood with her Uncle Edmund, their eyes met once again and a rush came over her. Everywhere around them melted away, drained of all color, except for Blaze bathed in liquid sunlight. Her feet left the floor. All motions slowed; sounds became dull as if the great lawn now sat at the bottom of a pool of still water.

Looking up she saw beams of light streaming down into the water. Yellow and red fish shimmered around her. Bubbles streamed out of her nose and mouth.

She swam into a vortex of which Blaze floated in the center. He looked at her and smiled. Air bubbles rose from his body, his limbs were lithe. In her mind, they reached for each other. He grasped her wrist and pulled her body to him, enveloping her in his arms. Their lips met while she floated beneath him. She breathed air into his mouth, his eyes closed. The electricity in their kiss rushed through her body; they engaged their tongues in a longing filled dance.

Her stepmother, Lady Katherine, broke her enchantment with a tug on her arm.

"Arose, Libby is missing, have you seen her?"

Arose gulped air while her mouth went dry. She stared at her shoes trying to think of an appropriate lie. "No, she helped me dress and went to dress herself, I suppose."

Lady Katherine clucked her tongue. "Well, with her off somewhere, you will have to set the platters for the wedding feast."

"Do you think I can stay out here for a while?" She gazed at Blaze's manly profile.

He caught her eye and smiling, raising his cup in a flirtatious toast. Lady Katherine quickly caught the exchange of looks. She took Arose's arm and led her in the opposite direction, toward the house, and pushed her though the door.

"I'm here to help Menga," she said, her lower lip in a slight pout.

Busy making dessert, Domenga looked wistfully at Arose while she whisked a bowl full of cracked eggs. Arose started placing slabs of hickory-smoked stock fish next to thick slices of polenta. Fragrant saffron rice and pheasants sat on trollies, ready for their trip to the Great Lawn.

"Rosie, where be da stone?" Domenga pointed her chest.

"The opalescent gem has been stolen." Arose bent her head until her chin rested upon her chest. She sighed out her breath and continued, "While I lay unconscious, a scoundrel stole it. Best I can tell a man named St. James, The Captain of the Red Spirit, took it from my neck last night." Arose's hot temper flared. She grabbed a large knife off the counter. "When I find him, he will give it back or I will cut him to ribbons!"

Domenga took the sharp blade out of Arose's hand and laughed. "I'm sure he will give it back to you," she said in a soothing voice.

"Don't be so sure—he is a pirate. I'm worried I may lose it forever. He is here at the party." Arose stuck her head out the open window, her eyes scanned the crowd. "I just have to find him."

Domenga's brow creased in concern. "You went out dressed as Evan last night. Danger 'ting you do. That new brother of yours went huntin' for you. You had best watch he don' catch you alone."

Arose's eyes widened and her breath stopped. The woman could see right through the new family member. What else might she know?

"Menga, Harold wants the Gem of the Red Spirit. He found me in the den and wanted it right there and then."

"Maybe it de reason why it vanished so sudden," she whispered. "The stone knows what is best for it. Don't be so quick to blame St. James."

"Yes, you may be right, but it's more than likely to be St. James. A thieving wretched pirate more than anything a gentleman or a ship's Captain," her grunts became almost incoherent. "Luckily Blaze, an old friend, wandered by and put an end to Ambrielle's advances." She sighed and her speech slowed. "Blaze is a very brave and honest man, everything Captain St. James is not," she hissed out his name.

"Do you want to see Blaze?" She said with a wide smile, a light shining in her eyes, "He is in the courtyard."

Arose took Domenga's hand and led her to the window. She pointed to a lively group.

"There, the sandy-haired man in the beige coat."

Many captivated women circled him; they gasped while he regaled them with a story. His presence stirred Arose, even at such a distance.

Domenga's eyes bulged from their sockets. Her entire body shook in laughter.

"Oh yes, dat be a brave one. He came through here to say hello."

"What is funny, Menga?"

"You will see." Domenga shook her head and went back to her work.

"I'm meaning to get myself out of here Menga. The sea is calling to me. There have been signs. I must come face to face with black-hearted Captain St. James. Only can I have the Gem of the Red Spirit again." She remembered what Reggie said. "St. James's porter told me that they are to set sail, to meet the captain in the Port of San Sabastian. If I can't find him here, I will have to travel there. But how, with Ambrielle watching me so closely?" she said, her chin tilted. "He seems to know my every move."

"It is safe where it is, and you have Mista Blaze to watch over you for now. You will find da stone when it is ready to come back."

When Arose returned to the party, she made her rounds. She greeted the ladies from town. She breezed by their husbands with a sly smile, watching their expressions while they lustfully stared her. She, the entire time, searched the crowd for St. James.

She spotted Blaze again. He smiled broadly while he spoke to the throng of enchanted ladies.

Strange, I thought St. James would be surrounded by women, and there is Blaze, charming them all. Blaze is the center of attention not St. James. Blaze...not St. James...why?

She closed in on the group, her eyes glued to Blaze, her thoughts coming together, that is, until Anne stopped her short.

"Arose, don't you dare approach him!" Anne stood between her and Blaze, her hands out blocking the way.

Arose jumped. "What? Who?"

"Why, Captain St. James, of course. Mother says he is to be my dinner partner, and you will keep your distance."

"St. James? Where? I have been looking for him all day."

"Don't make believe you don't know who he is. It is quite obvious you have been flirting with him all evening."

"Captain St. James?" Arose's head spun. "Where?"

"There, in the long beige coat." She jutted out her chin, pointing with it to Blaze. Arose stood motionless.

"Don't tell me you have never heard of Captain St. James and his ship the Red Spirit?" Her sister stepped back and blinked.

Not waiting for Arose to answer, Anne continued.

"Well, let me tell you." Anne took a deep breath. "He sails Uncle's flag ship and is one of the most wealthy and well known privateers on the seas."

"Blaze is Captain St. James?" Arose questioned, she brought her hand to her head; her heart pulsing blood gave her a sharp stabbing in her right temple.

Could there be two Captain St. James' in the world?

Arose pointed to her friend Blaze. Mischief flashed in his eyes when he spoke, reminding her of his expression while they played together on the ship.

Blaze...*the sea captain,* not Blaze the servant.

"Yes, Rosie. Captain... Blaze... St.... James." Anne said his name deliberately, emphasizing each word. She leaned in like a washwoman ready to share her gossip. "The word is, the ship is the most beautiful on the ocean. They say he had the ship made in the hopes it would bring his one and only love to him." Anne breathed finally. Arose fixed her stare on her sister, hanging on every word.

"And guess what?" Anne went on without stopping for an answer. "I intend on being his love." Anne giggled and did a quick leap in the air. "Rosie, are you being honest with me? I can't believe you have never heard of this. Where have you been all this time?"

"Busy, I have been busy," she said flatly. Anger welled up like a wildfire in her gut.

"Arose! What on earth got into you?"

"Nothing." She squinted her eyes until all that remained were perfectly curled lashes.

"I am begging you to keep your distance from him," pleaded Anne.

"Why, are you afraid I intend on stealing him or eating him?" she said in a hiss.

Arose's expression had changed so drastically in just a few moments. "A bit of both, I'm afraid," Anne said.

"At this point, either may happen."

Chapter Thirteen
The Exodus

She finally understood why every time she focused on finding St. James, she had to fight off flashes of Blaze's clear blue eyes. When she floated above him on the ship he managed to reached out and touch her cheek. She remembered the young boy Blaze wiping her tears away in much the same way. This was the reason she and the shadow in her visions were in such harmony, how she knew his aura, his spirit and his scent.

Why would he take her opalescent gem? Maybe turned by Morel, in some deep disturbing way. She had to speak to him without weakening, she had to be strong, her emotions stowed. She had to know how and why he took the Gem of the Red Spirit from her, not knowing if she could and would forgive him.

She and Anne stood on the great lawn in the burning sun. Her face flushed red and beads of sweat poured down the small of her back.

Anne's stern look mirrored her mother's. Very much alike in looks and demeanor, Anne's brown eyes burned when she confronted Arose. She pursed her lips, inspecting her sister, her hands on her hips.

"Rosie? What are you cooking up in your little head?"

"Nothing at all, Anne," Arose said innocently, although her expression betrayed. She gave Anne a quick glance from the corner of her eye. "So, Mother says he is to be your partner for dinner, aye?"

"We have not yet been presented to him, and I don't want you muddling anything up. Mother says you should keep away from him," Anne said defiantly folding her arms over her petite frame.

"She said that, did she? Well, let's just see."

Arose sped to where her mother stood next to Blaze. Anne chased behind her in a mad race to see who would reach him first. Anne was left to peek over her shoulder.

Lady Katherine scowled at Arose.

"Captain St. James? You already know Arose."

He gave her a rich smile and touched her hand with the tip of his finger. "Yes, I do, Lady Katherine, my dear Arose. How have you been?"

Be strong, Rosie. Be strong!

She melted, her mission all but forgotten. His crystal blue eyes met hers in a deeply meaningful way that only the two souls could understand. He kissed the back of her hand, moving closer to her, their bodies almost touching.

The warmth of his lips on her skin made her shiver. A tingle traveled up her arm and lingered a moment at the nape of her neck, like gentle kisses searching for a place to rest.

Something deep inside of her screamed,

Pull your sword! Sweep-kick his knee! Put him to the ground! The scabrous dog!

She opened her mouth to speak, to yell, to shout out her anger, but nothing came. She stood there dumbfounded for more than a moment, looking at him, searching for the right words to say.

Blaze shifted his weight from one leg to the other, smiling at Lady Katherine and back at her, waiting for her to speak.

The uncomfortable silence continued until Lady Katherine intervened.

"That's quite enough," she said. "Arose, you are looking foolish!"

She placed her hand on her stepdaughter's torso and pushed her behind her back, blocking her view of St. James. Her mother took Anne's arm and dragged her forward, bumping her into Blaze's barrel chest. "This is my daughter Anne. Anne, this is Captain Blaze St. James."

The captain looked down at Anne and placed his hand over his heart. "I am pleased to meet you, Miss Anne." Blaze stepped backward and took her hand with a deep bow.

"*Enchante, Capitiane.*" Anne almost melted into the folds of her skirt in an elegant bow, the training in the fine art of being a well-bred lady apparent. She smiled gently.

"I am hoping you can escort my daughter to dinner this evening."

"I would be delighted to, Katherine." He held out his arm. Everyone gasped and whispered when they realized he had meant Arose.

"Oh no, no, no. Arose is scheduled to be too busy to dine this evening. And Anne is more of your intellectual equal." Lady Katherine dismissed Arose with a wave of her hand.

Those in earshot let out a contemplative gasp. All eyes were on Arose to see her reaction.

"Ah. Maybe next time, Arose." He turned and held his arm out to Anne; she took it with a flourish for all to see.

"You had your chance." Her mother hissed at her when they were out of earshot of the crowd. "Ever since I came to this house you have been nothing but a thorn in my side. I tried to teach you how to be a lady but you never wanted to learn. Do you think all that reading and writing will find you a man? He wouldn't have anything to do with you. A fine Captain's lady you would make, you are more of a crewman." She stopped her verbal barrage. Lady Katherine tore down her wall brick after brick; she reached into Arose's chest and tore out what pieces were left of her wounded heart, and she knew it. She took a step back, her voice softening just a bit. "You had your chance with him—now its Anne's turn. Make yourself useful. Go find Libby." Her eye raked over Arose, inspecting her for the chinks the words left in her armor. If she meant to cause her any real damage, she had done her job, and now relaxed in her triumph.

Arose ran to the far end of the house, weeping. The lines and colors surrounding her became a watery blur of green and yellow. Her heart pounded in and out until she thought it would rip through her bodice and fall to the ground. Finding a secluded area between a hedgerow and the house, she stopped and leaned against the hot stones. She placed her head on a stone while the bitter tears streamed down her face. "Bess, I'm sorry, I am failing you!" It was more than just Bess troubling her. She was helpless for the first time in years. She had no one; she felt lost and very much alone.

Besides her sobs, she heard nothing and her only company was the chickens pecking seeds off the ground. The hot Jamaican wind blew at her. She looked around the scene, and she tried to memorize this time and place because she never wished to return to this dark place in her heart.

The bushes next to her moved. Before she could turn to see who it was a large hand covered her mouth. Yellow tobacco stained fingers muffled her scream.

Dragging her backward into the bush, Shaw Murphy held her tight against his body. She all but disappeared under his wide shoulders. He brought a dagger up to her face. "Don't scream, sweet darlin'. We don't want a mess here."

"Here, hyk hyk," laughed Faolan. He danced around the ground pointing. "Not here, but there or there or maybe there."

"Stop making jokes you idiot, tie her hands." Faolan smirked and pulled a rope from his jacket, wrapping it tightly around her wrists. Her hands immediately turned red. Shaw pulled out a cloth and shoved it into her mouth.

Liam, standing outside the bush, popped his head in. Her hands were turning a bright purple. "Do you have to be so rough on her? She's a lady!"

Holding her tight, Shaw looked, exasperated, at his brother. "Look at my face, Liam! She busted my nose. Just think what this bitch can do to you. She can take that skinny neck of yours and twist your head right off!"

Faolan, never wishing to be on his elder brother's bad side, spoke up. "Shut up, Liam. We have her tied. Bring the carriage here so we can git' er out of here." Faolan fired back. "Mother is waiting."

"W-w-what do you think mother will do to her?" Liam asked softly.

Faolan rolled his eyes. "What do you think she will do to her, maybe have some tea and sandwiches?"

"Yea, it will be Arose petal tea." Shaw laughed amused by his own joke.

Arose shook her head to Liam, her eyes pleading. Liam gazed down and shrugged his shoulders. He turned and disappeared.

A loud thud came from outside of the bush.

"Liam? Liam?" Shaw called and turned to Faolan. "Check to see what happened to him."

Faolan backed up to the wall. "I'm not going out there!" he said in a shaky voice.

Shaw squeezed her tighter, shaking his fist toward Faolan. "Go, you idiot." He kicked the dry dirt up at him. Faolan stomped his way through the bushes. Another thump came, then quiet.

Shaw slammed his back against the wall. "Faolan?" He waited a moment for an answer, "Liam?" Shaw sighed heavily. "Damn, where are ye'all?"

"Move it," he said impatiently. He pushed Arose in front of him, firmly holding her neck in the crook of his massive arm, until they came out into the light.

Blaze stood before them, but a very different Blaze than had held her hand and gazed gently at her just minutes before. His genial smile had vanished; a deadly seriousness gripped his face. His eyes held an anger Arose had only seen in her most intense visions, his eyes a gunmetal steel grey.

He had transformed into the St. James she saw on her spirit walk, someone who could be her equal in all ways, the man she knew she could love.

In the corner by the wall lay Faolan and Liam, unconscious.

"Let us pass or I will cut her!" Shaw gritted his teeth. He brought the dagger close to Arose's cheek.

Blaze's voice sounded low and grave. "Drop the knife and let her go."

"She is coming with me. We have a little score to settle, her and me." He squeezed her neck pulling her head close to him and licked her ear. Arose gasped for air and squeezed out a garbled noise through her closed throat.

With a sudden burst of speed, Blaze reached to his hips and pulled a rapier sword and a flintlock pistol from under his coat. Pointing them close to Shaw's face he repeated, "Let...her... go." His voice, threatening.

Shaw's eyes opened wide. He released the knife, letting it tumble out of his hand to the ground.

Arose dropped her head, and   slammed it back into Shaw's already blackened nose.

"Ahhhhhggghhh!" Shaw screamed in pain and released her. "You little bitch, my nose!" He stomped his feet holding his face. His legs buckled and he fell to the ground.

Arose ran toward Blaze and pulled the cloth out of her mouth. "Cut me loose."

Blaze cut the rope from her wrists. She rubbed her wrists and glared at Blaze.

She could hold back her rage no longer. She raised her hand and punched Blaze in the chest. "It's your fault! You took it from me! It's your fault!" Successive punches landed about his head and chest. He tried in vain to cover his face.

"What! Wait Rosie! What did I do?"

"The Gem, you idiot! You stole it, you bastard!"

Faolan and Liam started to revive. They crept over to Shaw.

Faolan whispered to Shaw, "She doesn't have it on her. Let's leave her here."

"Mother's not going to like this," Liam said in a singsong way.

They helped Shaw up, and with his arms around their necks, they slunk away.

Blaze dropped his weapons and grabbed her arms to stop the deluge of fists falling on him. Her hands now immobile, she kicked his legs until she finally found the prize and kicked him in his groin. He let go and fell to his knees in front of her, holding onto his crotch.

"Where is the great Cap'm St. James?" She walked behind him and glared at him crouching at her feet. "You have a lot of explaining to do, Blaze."

Blaze stayed on his knees in front of her. He looked up into her eyes, "Rosie, will you...please...explain what the hell you are talking about?"

Her voice shook, and she gasped for air, holding back her tears. "You took the Gem of the Red Spirit after you brought me, unconscious, to your ship last night. Admit you took it!" she screeched.

She put her hands up and pushed at his shoulders, barely touching him. He flew helplessly into the stones of the house.

Blaze slowly stood and began to limp away. "I should have let them have you! I saved them, not you."

"You're not going anywhere, St. James. She waved her hand behind him. He stopped in his tracks. "You owe me an explanation." He tried to move his feet but they wouldn't budge. She walked over to where he stood frozen in place. "Explain!"

"I penned a note for you before I left the ship this morning. I gave Reggie express instructions to be sure you read it first thing."

She looked at him blankly; her arms folded over her chest, a shield to protect her from the lies, deceit and general hurtfulness she had experienced since returning from her exile in Marmara. She looked away, hoping to block him out.

"I suppose you didn't read it."

She shook her head, speechless, watching his expressions closely. She heard Reggie's cockney voice in her memory. *"Pure Darjeeling." The teacup!*

"Was the note small enough to fit under a teacup?"

"Possibly, why?"

"Reggie kept trying to get me to try the tea. I thought it poisoned."

"Yes, he would do something like that. He is a hopeless romantic."

"What did the note say?"

Blaze looked straight into her eye. As if he had memorized every line, he began to recite the words that seemed to come to him so easy that morning before sunrise.

"My Dearest Arose,

"I will not bother you with the reasons I have taken your precious Gem of the Red Spirit, I am worried having such knowledge would restrict your movements, making you a prisoner of fear. You see I know you better than you even know yourself. I promise you I will return it to you when we are both safely on the Red Spirit. The spirit of the opalescent gem came to life as you slept. It begged me to keep you safe, to take the opalescent gem from you to save your life." Blaze stopped to take a breath. He raised his hand to halt her before she had a chance to offer any argument.

He continued, his voice so hushed she took a few steps toward him so she could catch each breath between words. "Suffice it to say in the moments before I removed it from you I witnessed your inner beauty, a vision most rarely seen in this world."

"I signed it—'Forever yours, Blaze St. James.'"

He shuddered for a moment, almost reliving the moments they shared while she was in spirit form.

"I didn't know what it meant at first but now seeing these blokes, I have to admit the spirit of the stone couldn't be more right. If you had it with you, I think they would have killed you." He looked off to where he knocked the brothers to the ground.

"The Spirit revealed itself to you? When did it do this?" She had never known it to disclose itself to anyone but her and Bess. She turned to walk a few steps away from him, her back to Blaze so he could not see her deep blush. She closed her eyes, already knowing what had happened in her heart.

"After you woke me—well, your essence woke me." A crooked smile on his lips told her he did not regret what had happened.

She flushed. "My spirit woke you. It wasn't a dream." Arose bit her lower lip, the ecstasy almost alive in her again.

"You came to me glowing, like a pearl. You were beautiful." He stared back at her. He reached up and touched her upper arm with the back of his fingers, dragging them slowly down the skin until reaching her hand. He entwined his fingers in hers.

"I thought I had dreamt it." She allowed him to wrap his arms around her, burying his face into the back of her neck.

"So you have known about the Red Spirit all this time?" Arose whispered. She closed her eyes, glad to know there was someone whom she can share her burden.

"Yes, I did. I have known about it since you were a child. My ship is named the Red Spirit, Arose." His eyes glistened as he spoke. "I have seen you come to me in your spirit form, flying above me, I reached out and touched your cheek. Your heart finally reached out to me, I knew you would be in some kind of danger. You needed me; I had to come for you, to protect you, as I promised Edmund all those years ago."

Arose felt her eyes begin to heat with the burn of tears. She smiled. "You kept my secret all this time. You are so dear to me." She looked down at their intertwined fingers, which rested on her hips. Lifting his hand, she pressed his fingers to her face. The feeling of his real flesh against the curve of her cheek took her breath away, and she knew she would never be able to breathe the same again.

Her mind snapped back to reality. She stiffened her back and her lip, her emotions snapping in line. "But I must have it back, now, I need to help Bessonth. I am weak without it."

"Weak? No, Arose, you are not weak. Even without the Gem of the Red Spirit you have incredible powers." He shook his head, "You haven't changed, Rosie. Can't help but pick a fight, can you?"

She passed her hand over his feet and released his frozen legs from the ground.

"The spirit is out of the opalescent gem. I must go back where it belongs, wrapped around my heart." Her eyes pleaded. "The silver thread that ties it to me is barely there."

"I will take you to the ship. You will have it by tomorrow." He spoke gently as he pulled her closer, whispering his words into her hair.

She gently pushed him away, "Ambrielle has a sister who is working all this voodoo magic. She wants to open the gates of hell to release the demons, so they can owe her their allegiance. She thinks she can control them." He looked at her strangely.

"Blaze, I have been there and let me tell you…there is no controlling them." She looked at him in dead silence. "If they are released, everything will become a wasteland, it will be Hell! And it will start right here…in Montego Bay."

"I have to get you back to the ship. Come away with me."

She turned her head as he slid his hand over her jaw to her neck, pushing her hair from the curve of her shoulder.

"It's not safe for you here. Let me take you away, let me protect you." He brought his lips to the nape of her neck. A warm breeze cooled the moisture he left as he swept the tip of his tongue over her silky skin.

"We will have to convince, Ambrielle…but yes."

Arose grabbed the soft lapel of his leather coat and brought him closer. Staring through him and into his soul she said, "Blaze, promise me you will return the opalescent gem to me." He gave her a silent nod. His hand reached under her chin, raising her lips to his. She closed her eyes, hoping to share a warm kiss. Blaze pressed his lips to her forehead. Her trust in him blossomed. In her heart, she knew she was safe.

Their bodies intertwined and a wind blew around them. A bright orange mist spun like a cyclone lingering while they embraced. The Red Spirit cast them in an invisible cloak. They stepped away from each other. The cloud dissipated and the spirit floated away.

They touched for a moment longer. "They can't see us come back at the same time," she said, looking deep into his crystalline eyes.

They smiled to each other when they crossed paths, her walking to the back of the great lawn and he toward the arbor.

She stopped for one last warning. "Don't touch the pewter pitcher; you will forget I ever existed."

"I don't think it is possible, Arose Du Mouchelle. You are in everything I am."

Chapter Fourteen
The Loan

The guests took seats under the grape arbor or under the white tents set up over tables. Anne spotted Blaze and sheepishly followed him to a busy table. To his left, Edmund sat with his feet stretched out and his arm resting upon the back of his chair. Libby, just returning from her tryst, lingered near. They played a flirting game from a distance. The place setting on the other side of Blaze stood empty.

Arose eyed the seat and made her way to the empty chair.

Jessup, a smallish child of about six, held his head low and pushed a large cart carrying a suckling pig. The little boy stepped on his open shoe buckle and fell flat on his face. The cart came to a sudden stop.

The partygoers laughed as the little boy stood. Tears ran down his dark cheeks, his lower lip quivering and small nose dripping. Arose knelt down in the path and held her arms out.

"Come here, Jessie." Jessup ran over to Arose's outstretched arms. She lifted the boy and carried him whimpering to the house. The "whoops" and "aww's" trailed off behind her as she handed the little child to Libby.

"Go with your momma now, and when it's time for bed, I will come and sing you to sleep. Would you like that?" The little boy nodded and reached for Libby who wiped the tears from his cheek.

When Arose returned to the party, her mother sat in the only remaining seat. She turned to Arose with a very self-satisfied smile.

"Ah, Katherine, how nice of you to join us," Edmund said loudly. He glancing back at Arose and shrugged, giving her a telltale grin.

She narrowed her eyes to him and stuck out her tongue. Edmund laughed with glee at the exchange of taunts with his niece. She knew her secrets were safe with him. She ripped a small sheet of paper off the gift table. She scribbled a quick note.

> *Dearest Uncle,*
> *I am in trouble yet again. Please help.*
> *Truly,*
> *Arose*
> *P.S. Do not drink from the pewter pitcher.*

Arose folded it carefully and called over a young servant. She pointed to Edmund. The child brought the note over.

While this was happening, Lady Katherine waved her hand to the servant who doled out droplets of wine from the talisman. "Some wine, Edmund?"

Edmund opened the note and read it intently.

He immediately placed his hand over the cup in front of him and looked up to Katherine.

"We won't be having any of that today, Morel." He blasted a look that went through Katherine and straight to Morel who used her like a puppet from her dank and fetid swamp. Morel waved her hand behind her. Katherine sent the servant away.

Morel screeched in anger and threw a full pouch of dust into Bessonth's fire. A ball of flame ensued, capturing her scream and sent it shooting into the heavens. The boom sounded over the music playing for the wedding guests. The string quartet stopped and looked into the clear velvet blue sky. The guests froze for a moment to see what would happen next.

Edmund looked up. "I think we are in for a bit of a tempest." He burst into a riotous laughter, a big toothy grin on his face. The strings began to play again, and the crowd resumed their conversations.

Arose hunted for a free seat. Her eccentric Aunt Josephine beckoned to her and pointed to a seat from which she had just removed her hat and handbag. Arose strode up to the chair next to Josephine's husband—her Uncle Louis. Arose grabbed a cup filled with rum punch and reluctantly sat down. Plopping into the chair, she sighed heavily and took a large swig from the cup.

"Too bad about the plantation, Rosie," her aunt announced when she sat down.

Remembering her next issue, she gasped, coughing when the liquor from her cup burned her throat.

"It's a sin you weren't built a boy, you know. Shame all the family's assets will remain bequeathed to an outsider." Josephine had developed no filter between her mind and her mouth. "But you do realize a woman running a plantation...owning property and such...just isn't done. Besides, you have no proper prospects for a husband in this town. Maybe if you can travel with us when we leave tonight with Captain St. James, you can find a man of your own."

She almost leapt out of her chair. "You are leaving tonight with Captain St. James?"

"Why yes. He just now invited us to sail on the Red Spirit. Captain St. James has been so gracious to offer us his stateroom. It's lovely, I hear."

Slumping, Arose let out a huge sigh. "Auntie, you have no idea."

"It is said he had the ship made to bring his love to him. Is it not romantic? I wonder who she could be."

"Yes, Anne told me all about it." She sank farther into her seat, then jumped up. "I can leave with you," she exclaimed. "Ambrielle wouldn't dare oppose my leaving if I am with you."

Her aunt blinked. "But, where are you going dear?" Obviously not listening to herself, her aunt was startled.

"I can go on holiday with you and Uncle Leo, of course! Are you leaving tonight? I have been working for weeks; I should have some gold coming to me."

Her uncle interjected, "Don't expect a farthing of gold from Ambrielle. He will be running the plantation and the refinery. While your father is of sound mind, the land is still his, unless, of course, your sister convinces him to sign everything over."

"What?" She stared at her uncle in disbelief.

Louis slowly shook his head. "There are plans afoot! Things will be different around here, Rosie. Wait and see."

Arose stood seething, arranged her skirt and walked over to the table where her father sat, partially drunk and very jovial. She gathered her control and took a deep breath before she sat down. She took his rough hand in hers.

"Father?" She sat across from him. "Uncle Louis and Aunt Josephine say Ambrielle will control the plantation from now on. Is that true?"

"Hello, Rosie! A good time had by all!" her father shouted. He lifted his cup and toasted all around.

The crowd around him responded with, "Salute!"

"Ahhh, Rosie...my dear sweet child. Life has not been easy for you, has it? I would like a dance with you, if I had a younger pair of legs." He began to doze again.

"Father, listen to me—are you giving the plantation to Ambrielle to run?"

"Yes, dear, everything now belongs to him; he is the husband of your elder sister."

Arose began her protest with "She is not my sis..." stopped short, knowing that saying the truth would get her nowhere. Her father adopted Fiona and Anne shortly after they came to live with them at Mason Du Mouchelle. To him, they were just as much his children as she. "What of your word? You told me I would run the plantation?" Arose felt kicked in the gut, all of his promises were empty now.

"You have, daughter, and have done very well here. Now we have a man to take care of things. Aren't you glad for this? You can go have a family of your own. And when I pass, he will own everything 'As of Right', like they say." He chuckled uncontrollably, amused by the reality of his own words.

Arose saw no reason for her to stay on the plantation another day. "I think it would be a perfect time for me to take a holiday. Aunt Josephine and Uncle Louis are travelling on the Red Spirit with Captain St. James. I would like to depart with them."

Her father patted her knee. "Maybe a holiday would do you some good, Rosie. You have been working too hard as of late."

Lady Katherine, within earshot of the conversation, interjected, "If anyone should go on holiday with Captain St. James, it should be Anne."

Everyone turned to look for Anne. Arose caught sight of her, quietly asleep in a corner. The little cask of rum propped up on her lap, a cup on the floor next to her.

Arose pointed. "I don't think Anne will be going anywhere for a while."

Blaze walked up behind her and smiled. "Did you have anything to do with that?" she whispered over her shoulder. Blaze looked over to Anne. "Well maybe, just a little."

Lady Katherine gasped and ran over to Anne and began to shake her shoulders furiously. Anne fell over onto her mother.

Arose covered her laugh with her hand and turned to Blaze.

Blaze bowed to François Du Mouchelle. "Sir, please, allow me to escort Arose on holiday. She will be treated with the greatest of care."

"Father, please, I need a holiday, I will be back soon." She lied, and although it bothered her to do so, she knew this would be her last chance to escape Ambrielle, his wicked thoughts, and his Voodoo priestess sister.

Her father sighed, "All right. I will miss you, my Rosie, but I will make arrangements with Ambrielle for some gold and a letter of credit." François turned and called to the new groom.

Harold Ambrielle stood in the corner, away from the other guests, still writing in a small book.

When Harold finally looked up, his displeased scowl made Arose extremely uncomfortable. He put the little book in a breast pocket and walked over to where she and her father sat.

"Arose is looking to take a little trip with Josephine and Louis. She will require a letter of credit and gold from you," her father announced.

"Well, I hope my dear sister won't be estranged from us for too long," he sneered at her. Arose turned her head away from his stare. "I'm sure we can come to some kind of agreement," he drawled. "She will have to make herself available to me when she returns," Harold Ambrielle said, scowling. "To, umm…" he hesitated and in a low voice said, "repay her expenses."

The words resonated in Arose's head. She shuddered at the thought of its double meaning.

Her father agreed, "Oh yes, yes. She will commence work immediately after she returns."

"I will give her the funds I see fit before the night is out." He fixed a glare on Arose, one that went right though her. "Sister, you must sign some papers to our agreement."

"Don't you trust me, Harold?" she snarled.

Harold laughed. "Yes, certainly, I do." The lie easily tripped off his tongue, but his sincerity was definitely lost in the tone of his words. Her father's head began to bob and a small snort sounded from his throat. She stood and gently kissed her father's head, lingering a moment to take in the sweet scent of his hair. She bowed slightly to Blaze and smiled.

Without another word, she walked triumphantly toward the back of the house. She sighed with cool relief—she would be one step closer to the return of her opalescent gem, and two steps farther from Harold and his relentless family. When she neared the back door, she lifted her skirt above her knees and dashed into the kitchen.

She passed Domenga who was giving the final additions to cups of warm coconut custards and pouring warm rum mixed with melted sugar, a rich, thick dark brown over them.

"Don't you want some dessert, me Rosie?" she asked. Busy at her work.

"No, thank you, Menga." She ran back to her. "I'm leaving tonight with Aunt Josephine to The Port of San Sabastian. I have to retrieve the Gem of the Red Spirit from the Red Spirit."

Menga asked, trying to take make sense of what was being said, "And the stone, Rosie?"

Arose continued, "It is there. Blaze put it away for safekeeping! When I'm done, I will be coming back here and rid the plantation of Ambrielle! If I'm not back within a fortnight, you, Libby and the baby get out." Arose hugged her nanny and ran to her room.

Menga laughed, deep and throaty. "Heh, heh, Captain Blaze, you don't know what you in fo'."

Smiling widely, Arose haphazardly threw clothes into her travel trunk and grabbed her leather satchel. Inside the satchel, she placed men's trousers and button down shirt. She stripped off the restrictive dress and corset, putting on some loose travel apparel and a leather coat to protect her from the night chill.

A knock came at her door. "Rosie, Auntie and Uncle are looking for you, come along." Fiona stood in the center of the hall, wringing her hands. Her white lace dress gleamed in the moonlight. "My Mr. Ambrielle is waiting for you in the drawing room. What is this all about?"

"Nothing much, just signing my life away." She slammed the top of the large trunk down and latched it closed.

She walked into the hall, dragging the heavy case behind her. "I'm ready," she said, and took a deep breath. "Fiona, are you sure about this Ambrielle fellow?"

"Oh, isn't he delightful? We will be so happy!" Fiona gushed.

"All right, Fiona." She saw that with her sister's innocence and the spell that had overpowered her, she was too far gone to listen. "Be a dear and call someone to bring my case to the carriage. Tell Uncle Louis I will meet them at the servants' quarters." She walked to the drawing room, putting on her leather gloves.

Arose stole a look behind her, Fiona had left the hall. She had disappeared from sight. The den sat between her and the door to the business office. She slid into the room where earlier Harold had her pinned to the wall. The dark parlor echoed the pain she felt in her heart.

Standing in the darkness, she tried to communicate with Bessonth in the bog.

"Bess, can you hear me?"

"Yes chil'." The dragon's voice spoke clearly in her mind.

"I am coming to help you. I will find the Gem of the Red Spirit I will free you of that prison you are in."

"You have to know dis Arose, Morel has put a curse on the tip of the Port of San Sabastian. She has set the land to quake if she does not receive the Gem of the Red Spirit

from you by tomorrow morning at 10:30. The port and everyone on it will sink into de sea." Bessonth paused; Arose held her breath, feeling she hadn't heard the worst of Morel's plan.

Bessonth continued, *"But if she does get the Gem of the Red Spirit, she will surely open the gates of Hell."*

Arose closed her eyes and fell into a vision of what would be if Morel had the opalescent gem. She saw Morel's thin fingers. In her palm, the Gem of the Red Spirit sparkled in a red sheen. The colors in the opalescent stone morphed continually, slowly churning inside the stone, until it turned a blood red. The spirit emerged from the stone, massive and angry. Its power insurmountable and unfathomably evil, it shot up into the sky where it burned a hole through the clouds and spread darkness in all directions. It returned to Morel and bound itself to her black heart. Morel laughed wickedly. As a spirit in the Astral Plane, she entered the gates of the Netherworld to be crowned queen over the demons. The darkness enveloped her, and demons closed in. A huge steely-toothed demon jumped on her from the crowd of undead. She screamed, writhing in pain, her empty soulless body stolen by a heartless demon when her essence was finally silenced.

On earth, dust rose up from the swamp, sunken-faced, wide-eyed people walked in death, while the round faced demons cut off the heads of the innocents.

"She has to be stopped," Arose whispered. "She hasn't a clue what she is about to unleash. I have seen her death. Maybe I can talk to her, maybe she will see reason."

"She will never listen to you, Rosie; her blood is too poisoned with hate. I have foreseen her fate long ago. I will try to make sense to her before I leave. When you arrive on the ship, obtain the opalescent gem, keep it safe, hold it to your heart and do not let her take it from you. You are much stronger than Morel can ever be." Bessonth's hopeful voice echoed in her ears.

Arose finally understood her choices. If she gave the Gem of the Red Spirit to Morel to save Bessonth and her family, she would open the gates of the underworld. The earth will become a wasteland of undead. If she kept the opalescent gem, Morel would unleash destruction on the Port of San Sabastian.

She made her decision—she must retrieve the opalescent gem and never let it go. She would be sacrificing the town, but at least they would have a chance to live.

"I will, Bess." She waited for a tense moment for a response.

Bessonth responded in a weak whisper.

"I will wait until you have the spirit safe wound around your heart. I will get out of dis prison and help you... I can talk no more, she is coming near." Hearing this, Arose began to shake. She reached up to her heart and felt the feather-light touch of the silver cord that connected her to the Gem of the Red Spirit, but thinner than before. Arose wondered how much longer she could hold out.

"Bessonth...stay safe." Getting no answer, Arose ran from the room.

She crossed the hall to the double doors, Edmund and Blaze stood at the far end of the room, having brandy. They watched her enter. She and Blaze traded looks; Ambrielle looked up and caught the exchange. He slammed a large ledger book closed on the desk. She had been keeping the ledger since she returned. On the cover, in her own swirling handwriting, it said "Du Mouchelle Refinery Co." Arose knew every number, every date and every name inside, what the company owed and what it spent. The pain of knowing this would be the last she would see of her work being more than she could tolerate; she closed and averted her eyes. The company would last five maybe six years before he bled it dry, she knew that for sure.

Ambrielle plopped down into a large chair; it creaked, the joints straining under his full weight. The new mahogany secretary desk, with ornately appointed legs and gold inlaid top, laid testament to the last few years of profit the business had since Arose's return from exile. It sat before a large window overlooking the expanse of cane. She clutched the leather satchel over her arm, smuggling her favorite dagger.

"You were looking for me, sir?" She curtseyed politely.

"Yes, Sister, you will put your mark on a contract. I will give you a loan that will be paid back on your return," her brother-in-law said. Ambrielle used his most deceptive ploy.

"I have worked without compensation all this time. I must have some funds owed to me." Arose looked down at her father.

"Do you mean to tell me you expect compensation, young lady? The only work suitable for a woman is prostitution." Ambrielle turned to her father and spoke in an authoritarian manner. "Is this true, Monsieur Du Mouchelle? If so, she must stand trial!"

"If this is your own opinion, Monsieur, keep it to yourself," Arose said with indignance, "There are many women who run businesses and own land."

Blaze drove a look at the overzealous Ambrielle, but Edmund placed a heavy hand on his shoulder and whispered in his ear, "She is doing fine, Blaze. Let her handle this buffoon."

He ignored her discourse and with his nose in the air said, "So what is it, Mademoiselle, did you or did you not prostitute yourself?" All eyes rested on her.

"Ten shillings." She kept her keen mind focused, ignoring the ploy.

Ambrielle squinted at her. "Seven."

"Nine and no less." She stared him in the eye, knowing his resolve reached its limit.

Ambrielle stammered, "Uh-uh. Done." Ambrielle opened the drawer and pulled out a bag of coins. Arose placed the bag on the platform of the weighted scale, and placed nine lead weights on the other side. The two sides leveled equally.

She picked up the feathered quill and quickly signed her name to the bottom of the note. Ambrielle threw the bag on the table where she stood. The heavy bag landed with a thump. She opened her satchel and placed it within.

"You see, Edmund! Sharp mind on that girl," her father exclaimed, gazing at her with admiring eyes.

"Yes, and that is why Ambrielle will fail." Arose adjusted the bag on her shoulder. "I would have gone down to seven, if you would have held out." All in the room laughed, all except Ambrielle.

Harold spoke bitterly. "Oh, and while you are on your hiatus, Mr. Du Mouchelle will be working in your stead." Her father attempted to stand and confront Ambrielle, but could not steady himself and fell back into the chair.

"No!" Arose yelled. "My father is not well!"

Blaze and Edmund voiced their opinions loudly. Blaze blurted, "See here, Ambrielle, this gentleman is way past the age of labor."

While Edmund's voice carried above the din. "I won't allow my brother to work a day for you, Ambrielle!"

"Well, it is all up to Arose. She should return quickly from her holiday or she may not have a father to return to." He turned his face to Arose. The boar's tusks and nose appeared and   faded.

Ambrielle sat back down. "You are all dismissed. I have a proposition to speak to Captain St. James about."

Edmund walked to his brother. "Come, François. I have no stomach for this man any longer."

"Dismissed, from my own office?" Arose's father said nothing more, staring blankly back at Ambrielle.

"You are tired, Brother. Get some rest." Edmund took him by the arm and led him out of the door.

Ambrielle laughed roundly. Arose turned and left her uncle and father standing in the hall. His voice echoed down the hallway, mocking her, following her outdoors to the night air.

Blaze approached the wood doors and stared at Edmund through gunmetal steel eyes that showed his anger.

He quietly closed the doors.

Blaze approached the desk. He brushed his long coat back, revealing a blunderbuss strapped to his leg. A longsword hung from his belt.

"What is on your mind, Ambrielle?" He crossed his arms, ready to pull his weapons.

Harold spoke as he stared out the window at the lush sugar plantation. "Your accent is very much like the new world. Have you ever been there?"

"I have been to a lot of places and speak many languages." Blaze shifted his weight, waiting for the moment he could end the conversation with a blast or a slice.

"Do you understand the language of deception?" Ambrielle scoffed while Blaze fingered the trigger of his weapon.

"What do you mean, Ambrielle?" Blaze's deep, gruff voice held an air of disdain.

"You see, I realize you fancy our little sister. But let me tell you she is not the angel you think she is." Ambrielle stood before the window looking out to the lush plantation.

"She and I were, let's call it, lovers, before I met her sister. What you saw in the den happened because she wished it, being her last attempt to continue our sordid affair. One last time she called it. She likes it… " Ambrielle paused a moment seeming to find the right words. "Well, she likes it, rough." He spun on his heels to face Blaze, lifting his chin to gaze down on him, looking for some kind of expression change.

Blaze remained indifferent. "If I remember correctly, you wanted something from her. What was that?"

"Oh yes, well, that leads me to my proposition. You see when we started our relations I gave her an amulet, a red opalescent gem. She wore it all the time. When she heard of my plans to wed her sister, she became incensed. If you have ever experienced her anger, you would know what I mean. She can be, ahem, unrelenting." Ambrielle paused, gazing out the window for a moment while he held back a breath. "I requested her give it back to me but she hid it. I have been begging her to return it for days on end now. I realize, at this point, I may require some help in retrieving it."

"What do you want from me, Ambrielle?" Blaze looked at him through narrowed gunmetal eyes.

"Ha ha ha. Yes, you, my friend, St. James, I am relying on you to salvage it, bringing it and her back to me, if possible. I am not without feelings for the girl."

"And what if she won't come?"

"Bring me back the bauble, St. James, I'm sure without it she would be despondent and probably try to kill herself. If she refuses to commit suicide, I'm sure you can make her death look like one?" Ambrielle drawled mercilessly.

"And what do I get out of this?" Blaze's curt voice cut the air, thick with murderous thoughts.

Ambrielle opened the lid to the secretary desk. He reached in and pulled out a bag of coin, twice the size of the bag he gave to Arose.

Blaze finally released the handle of the gun, staring down at the large bag on the table.

"Oh another thing, St. James. The funds she is holding." Blaze looked from the bag back to Ambielle.

"It is yours, whether she lives or not."

"This is a whole lot of money, Ambrielle." Blaze chuckled, shaking his head.

"It is! It is," he repeated, "but it is just to ensure the safety of our dear Arose."

He pulled out another bag and filled it with half the coin. Blaze watched him intently. Ambrielle placed it on the corner of the desk. Blaze walked to it and stared down. He picked up the bag and put it in his pocket.

"Overjoyed to have you on our side, St James," Harold drawled.

Blaze stopped at the door and without a word, exited the room. Edmund waited on the other side, leaning against the wall with his arms folded over his chest.

"What did he want?" Edmund asked as soon as he closed the door.

"Nothing, it's not important." Blaze averted his eyes and the two walked out to the stable.

Ambrielle poked his head outside the door. He walked into the empty kitchen and looked around pensively. Laughter came from the great lawn where his marriage party continued without him. Satisfied no one would hear him, he went to the dining room. There sat the pewter talisman. Immediately, Morel's image came to the side of the shining pewter.

The image spoke, "Well? Did he take the bait? Will St. James bring us the Gem of the Red Spirit?"

"I don't know, Morel. He didn't say he wouldn't, but he took the gold coin."

"You know for the Gem of the Red Spirit to work the cord that binds it to her must be severed or else I will never be able to have the full power over the stone."

"Well, I'm not sure I want that. I want her to come back and be there for me." Harold whined like a small child asking for another piece of cake.

"That can never happen, Harold. If she is not killed after the cord is severed, she will never be the same."

"Oh, all right." Harold put the pitcher back on the table. He blew out the candles and left the room.

Arose ran towards the servants' quarters and entered a small room. A tiny hay bed sat in the corner. Jessup sat up when she entered, his face scraped but healing. The moonlight streamed through cracks in the shanty's roof. His Sunday best hat sat atop his head and on his lap, he laid a red cloth. A few toys sat in the center including a carved pony and a cornhusk rag doll.

"Hi, Jessie baby," Arose cooed to the little boy.

"You leavin', Rosie?" His black eyes glinted, reflecting the light from the moon's glow. "Can I go wif' you?"

"I can have you come with me when you are older, just not yet." Arose choked, holding back her tears.

The little boy seemed to be appeased. "Sing to me, Rosie, please."

"Yes, yes, but first, can you do something for me?"

The little head nodded in agreement.

"Can you take this bag and keep it for me? Tomorrow morning at first light, you give it to Granny Menga. You, your momma and Menga get on out of here. But it has to be our secret, cross your heart?" The two traced an X on their chests, spit on their fingers and then touched them together.

She handed the bag to him. He hopped off the bed and crawled under. He lifted a floorboard and placed it inside a deep hole. She smiled, satisfied, knowing no one would find it and knowing she had just saved him from a taskmaster's lash.

"Thank you, Jessie. Okay, snuggle down while I sing to you." Arose hummed a low soft melody while her sleepy charge nodded off.

Chapter Fifteen
The Carriage Ride

June 6, 1692 10 PM

In the carriage house, Louis hitched the horses to the black lacquered buggy. He checked each horse the best he could, taking into account the amount of rum he'd had to drink. Bending over to reach under the horse's belly made the blood rush to his head. He stood with a snap and the world began to spin, taking the elderly man for a vicious ride. He took two steps back and fell into his wife, who had spent her time watching tapping her foot on the hay-covered floor.

"Odds-Bodkins, Louis! Be careful, you almost knocked me down!" Josephine's perturbed voice carried through the carriage house. "Where is the house driver? Maybe he could take us—you are way past the point of being able to drive a team all the way across the island."

"Don't worry, Josie my love, I have driven a team of horses much larger with much more to drink," Louis said.

"Dear, we have to keep up with Edmund and Blaze. They will be driving five hogsheads of sugar to the Port. Blaze looks like the adventurous type. I am afraid you won't be able to keep up and stay on the road. So I will worry if I like." She folded her arms over her chest and watched him check the bridles.

"Adventurous? Is what you'd call it?" Louis stood up, addressing his wife. "He seemed to be charming all the ladies at the party, especially your nieces. I hope he doesn't try anything fancy on you, or else I'll give him one of these in the mouth." Louis lifted his arm and threw a punch, spinning around and knocking himself to the ground.

"Oh, Louis!" she said, her fingers curled on her hips. "Look at you, all falling down drunk! I doubt I will be able to gain a bit of sleep on this trip at all!" She helped him to his feet and wiped the dust from his coat. "As if a strong handsome young man would have anything to do with me!"

Louise held her arm to help her climb into the ornate black carriage and closed the door. Blaze walked by the horses, taking his off his beige hat when he approached. He raked his fingers through his sandy blond hair, pushing it back out of his eyes.

Josephine popped her head out the window, starry-eyed when she caught sight of him. "Captain St. James!" she cooed. "We are so excited to be accompanying you on your journey."

Blaze smiled. "Yes, I am very glad to have you aboard." Blaze glanced over to an unfastened buckle under the horse's belly.

"Who hitched these horses?"

"I did!" Louis proudly announced.

Blaze bent down and tightened the strap without another word. Josephine eyed him, tilting her head to take in every inch of him. She pursed her lips when the muscles in his arms bulged under the restrictive sleeves of his leather coat.

Blaze stood up. "Would you do me the pleasure of allowing me to drive your carriage to the Port of San Sabastian?"

Josephine jumped before Louis had an opportunity to answer. "It's settled!" She clasped her hands together. "Thank you, Captain. We do have to pass by the servant's quarters and pick up my niece."

Blaze bowed graciously. "It shall be my pleasure, Madame."

"Thank you…Thank you, you are a good man." Louis's speech slurred as he held onto the cab for balance.

"Your coat is much thicker than mine, Louis. Can we switch just for the ride?" Blaze asked.

"Oh, of course, Captain!" Louis obligingly removed his coat and handed it to Blaze.

"And your hat there, sir, it looks more to the task than mine."

Louis had grown hesitant but handed his hat over to Blaze. "Yes, it does seem to be more of a carriage driver's hat than yours."

Blaze handed his coat and hat to Josephine. Outfitted in Louis's clothes, Blaze stepped back. Josephine admired the handsome man.

"Look at you, Captain. No one would know you were driving." Josephine laughed, clutching Blaze's things, brought them closer to her nose, inhaled deeply and sighed.

He stepped up into the driver's seat and settled in. Louise plopped into the seat next to Josephine. She wrapped her arm around his and rested her head on his shoulder.

"Settle in Josephine—it will be at least eight hours until we make it to the Port of San Sabastian." Louis spoke sweetly to his wife.

Blaze clicked his tongue and pulled out through the carriage house doors. He lifted the coat close to his face and pushed the hat down firmly on his head, peered out from under the brim. His eyes shifted left and right cautiously.

He drove the buggy up to the servants' quarters. Arose stood in the shadow of the doorway. The carriage came to a halt before the pathway to Jessup's door. She lifted her hood and silently climbed into the coach.

She gasped when she saw her Uncle Louis sitting across from her and looked back out the door window.

Meanwhile, the drowsy pair had already started to feel their liquor.

Arose shook her uncle. "Who is driving?"

He opened his eyes and stared blankly at her. "Captain St. James is driving the coach. Now rest your eyes. We will be in the Port of San Sabastian by daybreak."

Arose sat back into her chair and bit her lip, smiling slightly. Sounds of laughter and music from the wedding party illuminated the night. She breathed deeply, relaxing into the comfortable seat.

The lanterns strung between the trees allowed merry dancers to cast shadows along the ground. A pang of guilt thrummed through her body. She sat up, no longer able to rest easy. Yes, she had second thoughts about leaving her family in danger, but she would have a better chance to help everyone when Blaze returned the Gem of the Red Spirit to her.

Josephine snored soundly across from her. Her boozy breath filled the carriage with the scent of rum.

Arose strained to stay awake, but the rocking carriage soon took its toll on her also, and she drifted off into a dream-filled sleep.

Bright colors surrounded her; the grass felt soft under her bare feet. She sunk her toes deeply into the green blades. Sweet-scented wind filled her heart and soul. She felt herself swept away on the wind and flew over the ocean on the back of a winged centaur. Clinging to black dreaded tresses, she felt herself shake with fear of the unknown. Tears blurred her vision and stung her eyes. She searched desperately for the trouble ahead.

The air became cold from a northern wind, the grey sky rained down frozen pellets on her. A sunbeam broke through the blackened clouds and shone on a small blonde child, hanging precariously above a turbulent ocean. She dangled from the glove of a man. He kept her from falling from the edge of the high precipice onto the jagged rocks below.

"Hang on to me, Madeline! Hang on!" the man desperately called, while an evil cackle drifted in on the wind.

***

June 7, 1692 6:45 AM

The shouts deepened and smoothed. She struggled to wake up from her sleep.

Soon the carriage came to a halt. The town of the Port of San Sabastian's foggy air left dew on the carriage. Some of its people, still hazy from late night events, tried to make it home while others, with brighter eyes, were busy in their morning rituals.

A gloved hand extended into the open door of the coach, waiting for her to take it. She looked to see Blaze standing beside the carriage. Shaking, Arose took his hand and stepped out into the cool morning air, grabbing her satchel with her dagger and Evan's clothes.

"Morning, Miss!" Blaze's smile warmed his pleasant face.

Arose's dream had unnerved her. She felt the ground beneath her feet sucking her down. She looked down at her skirt.

Silvery translucent hands gripped her about her knees. Soulless bodies buried up to the shoulders attempted to pull her under with them. The sensation became too much for her to bear, and she fell into Blaze's arms.

"Please… bring me to the Gem of the Red Spirit," she whispered.

"Thank you for getting us here safely, Captain," Josephine interjected.

He nodded in understanding and released Arose. She took Josephine's arm and walked toward the carriage house.

A servant girl wearing a blue checkered apron threw feed to the chickens at a nearby coop. A large black bird stole a few seeds; a hen clucked madly at it. The little girl chased after the large bird, calling, "Shoo! Shoo!"

Arose smiled, watching the little girl. A bright light flashed in Arose's eyes. A stream of blood came from a large gash over the girl's brow.

She gasped and ran to her. "Someone, get me a cloth to stop the bleeding!" she cried.

She touched the girl's head, but the gash had vanished. Arose placed her hand under the child's chin and examined her face. The child's sweet face stared up at her quizzically. She backed away.

"Arose, you are acting quite odd this morning. What is wrong with you?" Josephine asked when she returned.

"Something is definitely off, Auntie. I feel something is about to happen. I have to get away from the Port of San Sabastian, the sooner the better."

Suddenly the thieving bird flew at them. They ducked to avoid it. It dodged at the last second, barely missing the pair. Screeching in alarm, it flew into a nearby tree. A murder of crows simultaneously took flight.

The huge flock sailed off in different directions, shouting a warning no human could understand.

"I believe the birds have the same idea," her aunt Josephine said jokingly.

Arose looked back at the black lacquered carriage. Louis watered the horses, but Blaze had disappeared.

Together they stepped down the stairs that led into the underground tavern, which doubled as a dining area for the carriage houseguests. Arose surveyed the room suspiciously.

A single candle on each table lent sparse light to the dank room; revelers remained from the night before. Drunken sleep had overcome more than one. Her aunt looked around the room with a displeased smirk. The bouncer roused some sleepy patrons and shooed them from a roomy booth. A server wiped the table with a dirty cloth. Aunt Josephine made her way over to it and swept the crumbs from the wooden seat.

Streams of sunlight shone through the panes of the red, blue, and green leaded glass windows. The light illuminated the flecks of dust swimming through the beams. Arose had been there a few times disguised as Evan. Worried she would be discovered as a woman, she watched the bartender pour strong coffee while an overseer stood in the corner eying her. She quickly pulled her hood closer to her face.

"How long do you think we will stay here, Auntie?" she asked, attempting to hide.

"I don't know, Arose. We have to wait until we can board the Red Spirit, probably just the day. In the meantime, we can catch some rest." Josephine searched Arose's face. "What is your rush?"

Arose's hands shook nervously. Heart pounding, she reached up to hold her amulet, but felt only the air-light touch of the disappearing cord. She placed her hand over her heart.

"This bad feeling won't go away. I saw the child bleeding from her head. The crows all flying off screeching told me there is something bad about to happen, I wish I had my amulet. The Gem of the Red Spirit would help me."

"What? Your pendant?" Josephine asked. "Did you lose it? Don't worry, it will turn up."

She turned and wandered off to the nearest table, Arose followed, taking the seat the most in shadow.

When they sat down, a young hostess came to their table, a white bonnet covering her fiery red hair. Arose knew the girl from her evenings there dressed as Evan.

She looked to Josephine. "Marm? A letter for your gentleman." Josephine took it and looked intently at the letter.

The young girl turned to Arose and looked into her eyes. "I'm sorry, Miss, but do you have a brother named Evan?"

"No!" Arose jumped at the girl.

The girl curtsied deeply and said, "Sorry Miss, no harm intended."

"It's all right, Annabelle." Arose bit her tongue when the girl's name popped out of her mouth.

Her aunt ignored the exchange and focused on the envelope instead.

"I don't recognize the hand."

Her aunt plopped it on the table, forgetting about it immediately. Arose scanned the parchment. She knew who it was from, having seen it only a few hours earlier on the letter of debt. It belonged to Harold Ambrielle. It lay on the table, unopened, in the dim light. Arose casually placed her gloves over the letter.

Blaze appeared next to them.

"I trust you ladies are being taken care of?"

"Yes, we are. Will you join us, Captain?" her aunt Josephine responded immediately. Blaze stood silent for a moment watching Arose. She grabbed her gloves and the letter intended for her uncle Louis.

"Excuse me," she mumbled and left the table.

Arose hid behind the wall and stood in the small stairwell leading to the common area. She urgently ripped into the sealed edge.

The letter read:

Dearest Uncle,

I regret to inform you Monsieur Du Mouchelle has fallen ill. I hate to dispute his claims of illness for there is no evidence other than shortness of breath and pains in his left arm, which come and go. I have no alternative than to have him declared incompetent and take possession of the Du Mouchelle Sugar Plantation & Refinery as right of succession.

Arose Du Mouchelle has placed me in a very precarious position. She must immediately return the monies she has taken or I will sell off shares of the plantation to keep the family in the standard of living they are accustomed to.

All "Free Black" servants must forfeit their status, to be full slaves. If they refuse, they must leave the property.

Please relay a message to Captain St. James; I am awaiting his answer to my inquiry. I remain in great hopes Arose will see reason and return to Le Mason de Ambrielle, her former residence. If she refuses, he is to do as I have directed him.

Sincerely,
Mister Harold Ambrielle

What is he planning with Blaze? Has Blaze gone mercenary? I should have known not to trust him. Is Blaze going to kill me?

Feeling betrayed, she tried to delve into his mind. A burning orange sun reflected off dark clouds, unintelligible voices hissed, suddenly a door slammed, blocking the vision.

Deciding to leave to the ship on her own to find the opalescent gem, she trudged out into the early morning air looking for her uncle's carriage.

Horseshoes thudded on the straw-covered earth when Arose entered the barn. She silently slipped in, closing the doors behind her, and changed into the black breeches and shirt she smuggled in her leather bag. She slid the shining dagger into its holster in her boot.

In the corner of the barn sat a covered wagon, still hitched to the horse. She crept up slowly and pulled back the tarp. Five barrels sat under the cover, all marked with the label "Du Mouchelle Sugar Refinery."

"Five hogsheads! This is what Josiah and the boys were after. This can bring a king's ransom in England," she muttered under her breath.

A low growl came from behind her. She turned slowly. Three wolves stood before her, their heads held low, saliva dripping from their jowls.

She froze for a moment, looking for a quick escape. Her heart pounded wildly. She stepped to the carriage and climbed up into the seat grabbing the reins.

The wolves closed in around her. The smallest snapped at her boot, catching its pointy tooth on the sole. She yanked her foot out of its mouth, pulling the tooth out, and bounced into the cart. The little wolf yelped and backed away, licking at the gaping hole in its teeth.

"Yaa!" she screamed and snapped the leather straps against the horse's back.

The horse reared up and whinnied loudly. Arose burst through the stable doors. The wolves followed behind, barking and snarling.

"Ya, ya!" yelled Arose to the horse cracking the whip over its head.

The just-waking townsfolk ran to their porches and balconies. They pointed at her as the wolves chased the cart.

The largest of the three sped past the others, in reach of Arose in moments. When she pulled back the reins to slow in the turn, the wolf took a leap at her, its snarling teeth getting closer. She turned the heavy whip to the weighted end hanging from her hand. She used it like a club and hit its grey muzzle. Blood spurted when the snout cracked. She pushed the wolf off the cart and it fell to the street in a heap.

A freckled boy watched, shaking, when the wolf thrown from the cart stood on wobbly legs, dazed, fell back down, blood and saliva dripping out of its mouth.

Blaze's face blanched when he caught sight of her while she whizzed by the tavern door.

"Untie that horse!" Blaze commanded to the boy and ran back into the tavern. He returned, slamming his sword into its sheath, his sidearm sticking out of his wide belt. The horse waited for him in front of the steps. In a bound, Blaze landed on the saddle and kicked his heels into its firm sides.

The skinny black wolf cut around behind the cart in one stride and leaped into the open back end. It climbed over the barrels until it reached Arose. Teeth skimmed her flesh as it snapped at the nape of her neck until it caught her by the shirt collar. Arose screamed when she felt herself pulled backward. The wolf tossed her into the air like a rag doll. She landed on the floor of the wood cart. With no driver, the horse ran blind. Dirt flew up behind the cart while the horse picked up speed, running downhill toward the docks.

The wolf climbed on top of her, snarling and dripping saliva over her face. She held the wild animal by the throat, digging her nails into its fur. It snapped at her face wildly. With a burst of strength, she heaved it over the barrels. It fell on its back on the farthest barrel and nearly fell out, if not for its long talon-like claws. The cart bumped aimlessly along the road as the wolf stalked up to her. It stopped before her while it savored its final lunge. Arose sat up and snatched a pointed dagger from her boot, ready this time to slit the wolf's belly.

Riding up and getting closer to the fast moving cart, Blaze kept his gun at the ready. He spotted the smallest wolf doing its best to keep in the midst of the fray. Blaze held onto the horse by his strong thighs, his musket clutched in his large gloved hands. He pulled up alongside the solitary wolf. His sharp eye gazed down the barrel and quickly pulled the trigger. The round ball struck the wolf running at full speed; it tumbled down the ditch into a rocky creek, mortally wounded.

The wolf on the cart stopped short and turned when the shot came. It jumped from the cart and ran down to where the small wolf lay dying. He sniffed at it and tried to move it with its muzzle. The small wolf looked up at the larger and whimpered. The blood flowed from its neck, spurting like a small spring. The water ran red when it mingled with the blood on its fur. Clear water pooled around the wolf like a dam and turned red as it poured over the wolf's body while it bled out. The head dropped to the ground, the young wolf losing its strength. It closed its eyes as it drifted off in death. The last of its blood swept down the creek.

The dark wolf stood silently over its dead pack member in the stream. Taking a deep breath, it let out a mournful howl from deep in its chest. It ran into the forest lining the road and headed inland.

The horse, spooked from the fracas, ran on. Blaze, closed in on the speeding cart. Arose decided in an instant that she would have to escape Blaze also. She jumped back into the driver's seat and looked for the reins. They bounced, hapless, along the ground. She reached down, almost catching them several times. Arose leaned dangerously down to the ground and caught them briefly but lost hold when the wheel hit a large rock. She sat up once more when the horse ran off the road into the thick grass. Going at breakneck speed, it headed directly toward a tree but veered off at the last moment to run under a low branch.

Arose closed her eyes and dove into the space under the seat. The branch swept over her head. Pain came from above her left eye, and she clamped her hand over a bleeding cut. The horse, tired from the chase, began to slow. Blaze finally caught up to the cart and pulled the reins back until it came to a halt.

He climbed into the cart, knelt beside her, and grabbed her wrist with a gloved hand. She buried her face between her knees, hiding from him, fearing a deathblow.

* * *

"Put your hands down!" he shouted.

Arose clamped her hands tighter around her head.

"Leave me alone! Don't touch me!"

"What is it now?" His eyes softened, the crystal blue in them sparkling like diamonds. "Let me see your head."

He hovered over her, his large chest obstructing the sun. She breathed heavily, holding back a deluge of tears.

"No, no!" she yowled. "Don't!"

He pried her fingers from her head. Blood spilled out and dripped down her cheek.

"Hold this!" He slapped her hand back to her bloody head.

"I told you!"

She gasped when Blaze reached into her leather bag and ripped her white pantaloons. He wadded up the cotton in his large hand and held it to the cut.

"How do you feel? How many fingers am I holding up?" He spoke calmly and held up three fingers.

"What stupid questions! Why are you trying to help me?"

"You are hurt. Be quiet, let me help." He continued to check to see if the bleeding had stopped.

"I read the letter from Harold. He said you and he had a plan. What does he mean? Are you trying to kill me?" she gushed, her voice trembling.

He looked her in the eye. "I am trying to help you now so I can kill you later. Does this make sense to you?"

"Maybe not...sss...ouch!" She hissed when Blaze removed the blood-soaked cloth. The bleeding had slowed. He sat back on his heels kneeling before her.

"Yea the scoundrel made me an offer, but I never even considered it. I almost killed him before he finished his first sentence. The fool gave me half upfront. If I wanted you dead, you'd be dead."

"Yes, I believe I would be." She snatched the bloody cloth out of his hand.

He held her under her chin, and looked deeply into her eyes. "I made a promise to Edmund long ago I would watch over you. That is a promise I will never break."

She stared at him.

He looked down at her, brushed her hair back from her face.

"Thank you." She gave him a quivering smile and breathed a sigh of relief to be comfortable in close quarters with him once again. "I'm scared, Blaze. I'm trying to be brave, I have to be brave for my family and Bess, but I'm really very scared." Tears ran down her cheeks.

He held her close. "I am here, and no one can hurt you."

"I'm not worried about that. I don't care about myself." She looked down. "What about Fiona? My father is sick! I cannot leave them in the hands of that man. He is taking the workers' freedom away, and I don't know what he and Morel will attempt with my mother and father. Hopefully Jessup and Domenga left this morning."

"What will happen if you give her the opalescent gem?"

"She is evil, and she wants the Gem of the Red Spirit wrapped around her wicked heart. All that power at her disposal. She would kill us all, and that will just be the beginning. She will open the gates of hell. Demons will pour out from the Astral Plane, consuming everything. Everyone, especially the small children, are in danger."

"You have to choose, Arose." His eyes were soft. "You have to choose if you will go back to the plantation and give her the Gem of the Red Spirit or keep it and come away with me."

"When the Gem of the Red Spirit is bound again to me, Bessonth will be able to free herself from the pit, and Morel will sink the town of the Port of San Sabastian below the sea. At 10:30 this morning, the quake will strike. Everyone here will die." Arose gulped and shook her head. "I can't let that happen."

"Maybe we can save the people of the town." Blaze pulled out the gold pocket watch from his jacket. "It's 8:43 now; we will get the townsfolk boarded on the ships moored in the harbor. We can head out to sea before the quake ever happens. Come away with me." He took her hand and placed it on his heart.

"Go away with you?" Her stomach flipped.

Blaze held her close and kissed her head.

"Yes, I will take you far from here, far from Morel, to where she can't find you."

"You have done too much for me already, Blaze. I can't put your life in danger anymore."

He pressed the palm of her hand to his lips, placing small kisses on the inside of her wrist. "Think on it, Rosie. I will help you any way you want—we are in this together."

She nodded her head gently. "Take me to the ship, Blaze. I need the Gem of the Red Spirit before Morel destroys the town with her curse."

She winced from the pain in her head. Blaze backed up, crawling on his knees until something crunched under him.

"What's this? Arose, did you lose a tooth?" He held up a small tooth in his hand.

"No, but I think the small wolf caught his tooth in my boot. Can I see it?"

Blaze placed the tooth in her palm.

She gazed down at it and gasped. "It's a human tooth, not a wolf's. Blaze, where is the wolf you shot?"

"It fell in the creek a ways' back. Why?"

"Show me!" Her voice wavered so much she could hardly speak.

Together they ran to where the dead wolf lay. Edmund knelt over a stream running red with blood. He stood when he heard them coming. He caught Arose in his arms before she reached the bloody scene.

"You don't need to see this, Arose. For Blaze's sake, you don't need to see."

Blaze's eyes opened wide and he knelt before the naked and bloodied body of Liam Murphy. "I shot a wolf, I didn't shoot a kid."

"It's not your fault, Blaze. Morel put a spell on him. She turned her own son into an animal. The fault is all on her," Edmund said, holding Arose.

Arose spoke, shaking. "It's true! I saw her put a spell on Harold. Bessonth said, the longer she stays Morel's captive, the stronger the priestess becomes. The biggest wolf...where is he?"

Edmund looked back up the road that lead to the town, "Last I saw, they were going to shoot it."

"I have to see."

Blaze stood. "We have to bring him back to town," he said, choking back his remorse. He took off his coat and with a swirl, laid it over the body. His coat melted down to the ground. The body of Liam Murphy faded away.

"What?" Blaze said in surprise. He grabbed the coat off the ground. Hundreds of small black bats sprang up from where the body had been. They encircled Blaze. Their wings hit his face and neck, pulling at his hair. Their cries deafened Arose, Blaze and Edmund. Blaze gritted his teeth and swatted at them as they swirled around him. He winced when their sharp teeth sunk into the flesh of his hands and arms. They flew higher and higher into the air and circled around, flying in groups here and there until they completed forming the face of an angry Morel.

She stared down at them, black features against a white cloudy sky. They turned and flew off, a black mass chasing each other over the forest, north toward the bog and Morel.

Chapter Sixteen
The Next Vessel

Time on Blaze's watch: 9:10 AM

"It wasn't your fault, Blaze," she said in his ear.

He nodded. A plain and simple response, just what she would expect from him. She watched his expression while they bounced up the road. Sadness gripped her heart. Arose placed her hand on his leg, closed her eyes, and connected with his soul. It seemed to comfort him, and he breathed a bit easier.

Arose spoke to Blaze in her mind. *"Are you better now, Blaze?"*

Blaze's head spun to look at her. "Yes, I am! How did you do that? How can I hear your thoughts?"

"The same way you saw me in the Astral Plane. We are soul mates. We have always had a special connection."

"Yes we have, Rosie, and we always will."

They travelled into the town in silence, their minds trading quips and barbs. Finally smiling, Blaze stopped in front of the tavern where the first wolf fell.

Blaze spoke to the men who were still crowded on the front porch still chattering about the early morning excitement. "Where have they taken the wolf?"

A big man pointed to the jailhouse at the end of the road. "They brought it there. Something's very weird about that thing."

Blaze tipped his hat and continued on to the dreary looking brick building on the outskirts of town. The sheriff came to the porch before they could get out of the carriage.

"Is this the one the wolf chased out of town?" The sheriff frowned as he looked down at her from his high porch.

"Yes, I guess." She squinted into the morning sun, "Can I see him?"

"Nope, he is too dangerous." He looked over to a brass spittoon and spat out a glob of black chaw. The spittle left a sticky line down his chin. He wiped it with a white hanky, then placed it into his pants pocket leaving a bulge where the wadded cloth sat under the material.

"Don't know what good it will do ya anyways. We just got our mind on bringing it out back an' shooting it, him being ravenous and all." He looked her over carefully. Arose squirmed in her seat.

"He's quiet now sitting in a cell, but I don't know how long we plan to keep him." The man spoke with a molasses-thick southern drawl.

Blaze and Arose looked at each other. His gaze settled her, her pounding heart slowed.

"I will keep him busy." Blaze telegraphed to her, his brow raised

"I can make my way round back, I'm sure no one is watching the door," she answered with a wink.

Blaze smiled and turned to the sheriff. "You from Louisiana?"

"Yes sir, I am," he said proudly. "You been there recently?" The sheriff smiled, his manner more congenial than before, Blaze's charm breaking down his surly barrier.

"We just came from there on my ship, the Red Spirit, maybe you've heard of her?" Blaze puffed out his chest.

"Nope." The sheriff spit out more black goo.

"Yea, ha ha." Blaze's voice went a pitch lower in embarrassment while his ears flushed.

Arose smirked and stifled a guffaw.

Blaze continued, "We traded some cane sugar for supplies at the docks. You sure you ain't never heard of her before?"

"Nope." The large man laughed deeply. "I hope along with some molasses for rum makin'." A twinkle came to his eye. "Did you get a chance to meet Red Jarreau while you were on the docks?"

"Yes, I know Red, the Dock Captain!" Blaze exclaimed. "Nice guy, nice guy," he repeated himself thoughtfully. "Him and his buddy...Jose Galvez and I threw a few back at the Black Smith Tavern in the Quarter! What is your name, friend? I will tell Red I saw ye here."

He elbowed Arose. She lowered her voice and sat farther apart from Blaze. "You have an outhouse here, Mister?"

"Ya, the privy is around back," the sheriff said, without giving her a second glance. "Jahn Richardson is the name. Pleased ta meet ya." He stuck out his huge hand to Blaze. "What your name be, son?"

She jumped down from the cart while Blaze and Sheriff Richardson were deep in conversation.

"St. James, Blaze St. James."

She turned and stomped down the dusty path to the back of the building. She found the back door and as she expected, she found it unlocked. Slipping in, she passed two, and then three cells. In one, a drunk snored soundly, lying on a wood bench with a bucket nearby.

Finally, she found the large wolf with the broken snout. It paced in the jail cell. His head hung low, bloody saliva dripping from its jaws. Deep growls emanated from his chest while a thick line of blue-gray fur raised down in the center of its back. Arose approached the cell cautiously.

"Shaw Murphy," Arose said flatly. The wolf turned and leaped at her. Startled, she gasped and stepped back out of his reach. He slammed against the bars and dropped to the floor. She stood breathing heavily, clutching her chest, studying the still body spread out like a rug before her. Not moving for more than a moment, he dazedly stood and skulked away. She detected an air of satisfaction around the animal, his growl turning into a staccato chuckle.

Fear making her gut wrench, she stepped forward again. Holding her breath, she lifted her chin to brace her resolve. The wolf sat staring at her with steely eyes, curled up, his body heaving and writhing while he let out small whimpers that drew Arose's pity.

The brown and grey hair on his body seeped into his skin. Black claws blanched and shrunk into his fingertips. His ears rounded and his snout flattened into his face. Pale skin grew over splitting flesh, which formed into a new body, shining with cold sweat. When he gained balance, he stood up on his hind legs. Crackling bones crunched and ground together as they converted into the skeleton of a man. Muscle torn from bone regrew immediately as ankles, knees and shoulders sprouted out of the wolf's contorting body. Its growls turned into pain-soaked grunts, when jowls and chin protruded from massive shoulders. Naked, the still-transforming body of Shaw Murphy stood before her. Blood from his beaten nose caked around his mouth. He cracked his neck and leered at her.

"You broke my nose again, bitch."

"I want you to know your brother Liam is dead."

He ignored the sullen news, as if he already knew. He looked up at her bloody head, her hair matted over the open wound.

"Did Faolan split your head open?" he said finally with a chuckle.

"No, he went running back to Momma as soon as he saw Liam dead on the side of the road."

Shaw said nothing but looked away from her gaze, hiding tears welling in his eyes. He spat out blood, which landed next to her foot.

"Liam didn't have to die, Shaw. He was just a kid! I know you pushed him into all this," she said, her voice trembling. "You and your mother are to blame for his death. Why, Shaw? Why?"

Shaw wiped tears from his face and after a breath said, "The stone, she wants the stone! It's all she cares about. She don't care about Liam! Not Faolan or me! Just the damn stone." Bitterness filled his tone.

He paused and stared out the window across from his iron room.

"Morel was to be the next vessel of the Gem of the Red Spirit. Bess had promised it to her when she came of age, before you were ever born. She backed out at the last minute, saying Morel hid a dark side." He turned his face up to the ceiling, hiding the pain. "If Bess had given her the stone, things would have been different."

He looked at Arose; his eyes laid the blame on her for years of abuse and neglect.

"Maybe if Old Bess had given it to her she would have been good. A good person, a good wife." He paused. "A GOOD MOTHER!" He screamed in pain, rattling the bars of his cage. Tears flowed freely from his eyes now. He let his head drop with a thud onto the bars. "Maybe Liam wouldn't be dead right now. A real upright kid, ya know? He would have been better…better than me at least." He breathed slowly, regaining his calm. "Now she wants what Old Bess promised to her years ago. You have no idea what the Spirit can do. Only Morel can bring it to its most powerful."

Arose calmed her voice, "If she goes through with her plan, she will be killed by the demons in the Netherworld. No one should ever open the gates. They are stronger than she is. I'm trying to save her life too here, Shaw. Do you think you can help me?"

Shaw scoffed. "It's too late. While she holds Bessonth, you are at her mercy. If the dragon escapes, the deal will be broken, and this town will come crashing down at 10:30 and there will be no way for you to stop it."

Bessonth! The threat made her shake. She took a deep breath and calmed. "Morel is a leech, doing nothing more than sucking on Bessonth's magic. Without her, Morel will be powerless," she said flatly.

"Give up the stone, and no one else will be hurt." He licked his wet lips. "If you return to the mansion and give up to Harold, the town won't be destroyed. He may just even take you back. I can see why, but you'll be….ha." He stopped short and chuckled. "Well, let's just say you won't care anymore. So it won't matter what he does."

He seared a look down at her. "The silver cord still binds the spirit to you. Right?"

She touched her chest and felt the feather-light, silver cord. "Yes," she said innocently.

"It must be completely severed. It is the only way Morel can have control over the Gem of the Red Spirit."

Steel grew in her resolve. She jumped at him and spat out her words, "She will never control the Red Spirit, Shaw. And you will most probably be shot before you can try anything else."

"Do you think she would only send the three of us to get you and pretty boy Blaze?"

A sudden realization came over her. Harold Ambrielle had to be there. She looked out the window into the brush for the large lurking boar. Seeing nothing, she turned back.

"Listen, Shaw. I am going to find the Gem of the Red Spirit. You, your mother, and your uncle had better watch out." Her deeply intense tone showed a vengeance she had never felt before.

Shaw pressed his body against the bars. His arm transformed instantly. He reached out for her with a hairy paw. Wolf claws missed her face by inches. His actions showed her more than she wanted to know. She turned and ran from the jail. Still deep in conversation with the sheriff, Blaze stepped back when she ran past and leaped into the cart.

"Take me to the ship now!" she said, not willing to wait a moment longer.

Blaze tipped his hat to the sheriff. "Nice meeting you, Jahn."

She grabbed the reins and released the brake. The cart turned, and she snapped the leather straps on the horses back. She raced down the road toward the docks.

They quickly approached the curve in the road where she lost control the last time. Blaze grabbed the reins and controlled the horse skillfully, keeping the heavily laden cart on the road. They rode on in silence. Blaze studied her profile.

"What happened in there?" he shouted over the rushing wind.

"Ambrielle—he is here," she said, concentrating on the road.

"The wolf told you this?" Blaze stared at her, his voice tinged with disbelief.

"The wolf transformed into Shaw, the dead kid's older brother. They are Morel's sons."

Blaze sat in silence.

***

Time on Blaze's watch: 9:40 AM

They approached the dock at breakneck speed.

The water's depth around the Port of San Sabastian allowed even the largest ships to pull up right to pier. Moored at the farthest slip, the Red Spirit moved to the rhythm of the rolling tide.

When Blaze finally stopped the cart, Arose jumped off and headed to the wood gangplank.

Blaze ran up after her, calling for his porter, "Reggie! Reggie! Where are ye, man?"

He bounded down the narrow stairs into the galley. There they found Reggie cleaning some silver, seemingly oblivious to Blaze's shouts.

"Oh 'ello Cap'm!" His cheeks turned crimson when Arose entered the doorway. "'Ello again, Miss," he said shyly.

Arose smiled at Reggie. "Hello Reggie. Glad to see you made it back on board all right."

"Reggie, where is Arose's necklace?" Blaze's stern voice had an edge of kindness for the old man.

"Oh yes, y-y-yes. This way, this way." Reggie beckoned to them, leading them down the hall while he spoke. A nervous stutter reverberated in his voice.

Walking through the narrow hallway, Blaze and Arose moved closer together. Blaze reached for her hand and pulled her along. Self-assurance thrummed down his arm into her body. Her pulse slowed, her rapid breath came more even. The Gem of the Red Spirit's nearness calmed her. She felt the warmth of its presence. Reggie led them into Blaze's quarters. Behind a desk, a nondescript nautical clock decorated the wall.

"I figured the lady would come looking for it soon, so I placed it here for safe keeping."

He took a winding key from a ring on his belt. He rattled the keys in his shaky hand. The jangle unnerved Arose. The clock placed high above his head, Reggie, with his short stature, had to stand on his toes to reach it. He put the key into its face to wind the gears. He slowly turned the key counter-clockwise three times. With a click, it unlocked and the face popped open. The red-orange glow of the opalescent gem's spirit leaped out. The gleaming Gem of the Red Spirit sat inside the clock waiting for her. When Blaze pulled it out, Arose smiled and stared into the precious gem. The red illusion moved quickly around the dome of the opalescent gem. Blaze held it by the delicate chain over her head. Arose closed her eyes and turned her back, waiting for the magic to begin.

Her sensations heightened as a numbing chill cascaded through her body. A hand around her throat squeezed tight.

She opened her eyes to find Ambrielle before her, holding her by the neck, a dagger pointed at Blaze's throat. Blaze moved back and pulled his sword from its sheath. From behind him, the edge of a blue and white porcelain vase poked up above Blaze. It slammed with a crushing blow over his head. Blaze crumpled to the floor, taking with him the Gem of the Red Spirit.

Reggie stood there, the end of the smashed vase in his hand.

"So sorry, Cap'm!" Reggie said to Blaze, lying unconscious on the floor. Looking up at Ambrielle and Arose, he said, "Take the girl and the gem and get off the Red Spirit! You have what you want. I lived up to my end of the bargain. Now leave."

Arose stared at Reggie. "Reggie! No… Please!" she begged, Ambrielle choking the breath from her.

Harold Ambrielle picked up the Gem of the Red Spirit. Smiling smugly, he looked into the opalescent gem's spectral dome.

"Tie him up and cast off. I don't want any more interference from him. Next time he will be dead," Harold Ambrielle snarled at Reggie. "Here's a trifle for your trouble." He put the amulet in his pocket and pulled out a small bag of coins. He tossed it to the servant. "Buy yourself a pair of decent britches."

Reggie looked down at his pants and shrugged. He knelt beside Blaze and held his hand.

***

Time on Blaze's watch 10:17 AM

Holding Arose by the arm, Ambrielle dragged her from the room and walked to the top deck. Wind blew across the bow, making the ship pitch and moan against the pier.

"I will take you home and you will be my mistress." He opened his mouth and stuck his thick tongue in through her closed teeth, enveloping her lips, including most of her face. She jerked away and wiped her mouth with her forearm. Glaring, she slapped him hard across his jowls, sending him back a step.

He righted himself, holding his jaw.

"You will be mine!" he screamed into her face.

Arose spat at him. He wiped her spittle off with the back of his hand, and   slapped her hard on the cheek.

He took a rope out of his pocket and wrapped her hands tightly, pushed her down the gangplank. Going headfirst over the edge, she held her breath expecting to slam into the water below.

She felt an arm wrap around her waist and found herself standing upright again on the incline. Looking behind her, she saw Harold's face frozen in fear. He let her out of his grip. They continued down the ramp slower this time, him guiding her carefully, his hand on the small of her back.

"Thank you," she whispered over her shoulder. He nodded silently.

Farther down the dock, three men were busy at the cart. They picked up the tarp covering the hogsheads of sugar bound for the Red Spirit.

"Here it is, guys. Nary even an eye watching," Simon called.

"Let's get in and get out of here before anyone sees us," Josiah whispered, looking around, gingerly climbing into the cart.

"Don't look now, Josiah, but there are two people coming down the plank," Leon said.

"Hey, it's not a people! That's Evan!" said Simon happily. "Hi Evan!" He called to her, waving his hand frantically.

Arose looked up and waved, showing them her binds.

"Who is behind him? He's got Evan tied up." Leon grabbed his dagger.

Josiah pulled out the rusty blunderbuss, and the three met them on the foot of the ramp.

"Hey you, leave him alone!" Leon shouted.

Harold Ambrielle stared at them blankly. "Him? Do you think this is a man?" He pulled Arose's blouse open, exposing most of her breast and the beauty mark on it. He pulled her hair out of its tie. It tumbled over her shoulders.

"Rosie?" Josiah blinked at her.

"I knew it, I knew it! I knew Evan was Arose all along." Leon stomped his foot on the ground.

Simon turned to Leon and said, "Well, why didn't you let us in on the secret?"

"What do you think of your friend now?" Ambrielle cackled, triumphant.

Josiah narrowed his eyes and tipped his head off to the side. "I'll tell you what I think. I'll tell you this…"

He put up the gun and aimed carefully. She jumped to the side before Josiah squeezed off a shot, striking Ambrielle in the shoulder.

"Get him, guys!" Leon cut Arose free, then leaped into the fray with his friends. "Raaaah!" the three screamed, rushing the man twice their size, knocking him to the ground. Ambrielle's cape covered him completely. The mound under the cape stopped moving. Raising his arms in triumph, Simon climbed on his back and sat all his weight on the still mass. He bounced up and down like a child, playing king of the hill. They congratulated each other, patting one another on the back.

***

Cloth ripped under the cloak, the body vibrated, and exploded upward. Harold the boar snorted violently. Tusks the size of barrelheads sprouted from his face.

Thrown up and away, Simon landed on a nearby stack of crates. The boar grunted, wildly thrashing around. Ripped and bloody, Ambrielle's clothes flew into the air. Arose watched the opalescent gem, thrown from his pocket, bounce away from them, heading directly toward the water. Arose leaped at it, and her fingertips grazed the amulet. The Gem of the Red Spirit hit the water with a small plunk.

The boar looked at her with blood-red eyes and charged.

Arose crouched over the landing and dove into the murky water. Her ears popped while she swam deeper and deeper into the brackishness. Finally, an orange glow showed her the way. She reached out for the Gem of the Red Spirit as the last of her breath bubbled up out of her nose. Grabbing it from the abyss, she clasped it tightly in her hand, held it to her chest like Bess had done when she first bound to the opalescent gem. An orange funnel surrounded her. She heard Bessonth's voice mumbling out ancient words. Her heart opened and once again, the Red Spirit entered and bound itself tightly to her with the infinite silver cord.

Finally able to breathe under the water, Arose called out to the dragon, "Bessonth! I have it!"

"Now chil'. It is time for me to break free," Bessonth said.

***

June 7, 1692 10:30 AM

The quake made its first rumblings when Arose hit the surface. She attempted to clutch the wavering pier, but she kept slipping off the slick braces, falling back into the water each time. Arose reached out her hand, searching for a solid support. An abrupt, clean fast jerk pulled her out of the water.

Blaze clutched her soaking body in his arms, his chest throbbing with the beat of his heart. She looked at him and beamed. He kissed her quick and hard.

"What happened? I thought you were knocked out," she said, overjoyed to see him.

"Arose, don't you know by now, nothing will keep me from you ever again," Blaze said while he steadied himself on the rocking pier.

Arose breathed deeply and held her head against his chest. She closed her eyes for just a moment.

They jumped when a blood-curdling roar came from behind them.

The boar had chased Leon, Simon, and Josiah up the highest stack of crates on the dock. "Run back to town and warn as many as you can. Send them to the ships. I will take care of this one." Blaze's clear blue eyes glared at the grunting boar.

Seeing the two lovers holding each other, the boar charged. Arose held the opalescent gem tightly and disappeared. Blaze stood alone, his razor sharp sword in his fist.

Arose leaped over the charging boar unseen and ran with all her strength. The road rushed under her, down into the center of the town.

Chapter Seventeen
Dragon's Day

Arose went to find Uncle Edmund. He peered up at a window on the second floor of a brightly painted green house. She stopped short and slowly walked up to the surreal scene. The once pristine home leaned precariously to the left. Crumbled bricks and wood blocked off the front doorway. The front porch, a palace of beige and rose pink columns, had splintered into shards, the points sharp and ready to impale. The collapsed ceiling crushed wicker chairs and baskets of colorful flowers. Ready to consume the beautiful home, fire and smoke billowed from the kitchen window.

Edmund stood with his arms outstretched and called up to a man who paced in front of an open window.

"Drop her down to me if the stairs are caved in, I will catch her!"

The man in the window dropped a small bundle down to Edmund's waiting hands.

He cradled an infant in his arms.

Arose exhaled when she heard the child yowl and approached. "Uncle, send them to the docks, the Red Spirit will take us to safety."

"Aye, me girl, we will all be saved, if the ship can outrun the big wave." Edmund looked out into the distance. A whitish pallor came to his skin.

"The big wave?"

"Yes, I have seen it with me own eyes, child, when the land rose under the seabed off the farthest isles of the Japans. The world rumbled as the town fell before us. Roads turned to quicksand under our feet. The ocean stood calm for a while. Then the worst of it happened. As if the voracious goddesses of the sea Scylla, Charybdis and Thetis, stood side by side in retribution. All angered by the gods of the underworld for encroaching in on their domain. They sucked up the water into their mighty lungs, and when they were ready, spat out seas, sending wave after wave of water, some twice the size of this here building." He turned and pointed to the tall building with his chin. "The water covered the island, up to twenty miles inland. The Japanese called it *tsunami*." He breathed heavily. "You see, me darling, tis not the quakes which can kill us as much as the wall of water which will come after. If we are anywhere near land when it falls we can end up hundreds of kilometers inland... smashed to bits."

She looked into his mind; the rolling seas were black with churning soil and littered with bodies, rolling ever-farther inland. A chill ran up her spine.

Arose backed away. "Blaze will have to outrun it. If not, I have a standby plan."

"You had better. If we are near land, there is no way to outrun it." He shouted while she ran from him, "We have one turn of the clock Arose, just one!"

He handed the infant to her terror-stricken mother who, awestruck, listened to his story. Gravely, he looked at her and said, "Head to the docks, there is a ship waiting."

The mother nodded and grabbed the arm of a small child. She rushed down the street while her two other children followed.

Arose ran back to the tavern and went down to the bar area. There she found her Uncle Louis, standing alone, holding a mug aloft.

"Here's to those who wish us well. All the rest can head to..." a small tremor came, dust from the ceiling showered down on him. "...well, you know the bloody rest." He took a slug of his ale and turned to Arose when she came in.

"Where's Aunt Josephine?" Her voice shook.

"Under there." He pointed to a long table in a dark corner. Her Aunt Josephine hid, squashed between the legs of the wooden slab. Her skirt rumpled over her face.

Arose ducked her head under and peered in at her petrified aunt.

"Auntie! You must come with me!"

"No! No, you come under." Josephine stuck her hand out, trying to grasp Arose by her ankles.

Arose caught Josephine's hand and tugged her out from her hiding place.

"Auntie, please come! Blaze is waiting for us at the dock. We have to cast off before all this is under water." Grabbing her uncle by the shoulder, she pushed them in front of her. She managed to get them up the stairs, urging them on with every step through the narrow hall.

Her uncle walked to the door and stopped. Digging through his pockets. Arose and Josephine collided into him.

"I have to pay me tab!" He turned and tried to pass them in the small dusty hallway, heading back into the underground bar.

"Your tab? Oh dear Lord!" Arose sensed another tremor ready to hit. The walls creaked, about to give way. She grabbed the coins out of his hand and threw them down the staircase.

"My change!" he said as Arose pushed him to the door.

"A tip, leave it as a tip! Please, Uncle, we have to hurry! The building is about to come down!" Uncle Louis nodded and Arose managed to get them out of the building.

The ceiling of the underground room caved in as they ran out to the middle of the street. The rest of the two-story building followed, leaving nothing but broken pieces of wood and dust. The fire burning in the hearth spread quickly through the dry tinder.

Soon, engulfed in flames, the splintered remains of the inn sent enough smoke, soot and fine dust into the air to blot out the sun. It hung like a low-lying fog. People were running this way and that, like mindless stampeding animals looking for a way out. Squawking chickens tried to take wing as a fissure developed down the center of the road.

Arose remembered the little girl who fed them, her sweet face looking at her with confusion in her eyes. A high-pitched scream caught her attention. She turned to see the same child standing under a shaky balcony. In front of her, sandy dirt poured into the crack in the road. Frozen in place, the child didn't dare move.

Everything around Arose blurred as she sprang into the air and flipped over the fault to reach the frightened girl. Arose scooped her up and leapt back across the widening divide. The balcony crashed down to where they had stood seconds before. She handed the child to Louis who hung onto her, glancing at the child   back up to Arose.

"How did you do that?" Aunt Josephine asked.

"Doesn't matter, the child is fine now." Arose passed her hand over the little girl's head, happy that she was there in time to save her.

"Take her to the Red Spirit. There is someone I have to speak with." Her uncle nodded and headed down the road holding the child in his arms, her feet bobbing as they ran.

She stared down the collapsing road before her.

She had only moments before the earth beneath her feet liquefied and sucked her under. She took off running, pushing herself through her pounding heart, to run faster as she headed for the jailhouse.

When another tremor hit, glass from buildings exploded into the streets. Fires broke out while smoke and dust bellowed out from everywhere. Townsfolk pushed and shoved as they pulled their prize possessions behind them.

People still inside their homes screamed as the walls collapsed in on them.

She stood at the doorway to the jailhouse for a moment to observe the town.

"Morel will pay for this curse," she murmured.

When she entered the jailhouse, the sheriff rushed to open the cells and shouted at the inmates. Occupants collected their things and ran out the door. He walked into the old drunk's cell, lifted him, still sleeping throughout the tremendous rumblings. He stopped in his tracks when he spotted Arose. "What are you doing here, girl?"

"Give me the key to the wolf's cell," she said pointing.

"Time to evacuate, it's just a durn wolf, git yourself to safety." The sheriff looked at her in disbelief.

She held out her hand stubbornly, stoic determination on her face. Jahn Richardson threw her the master key.

"You're a crazy one," he murmured as he ran out the door, the old drunk swaying on his back.

Arose went to Shaw Murphy's cell. The wolf paced frantically inside. She slipped the key into the lock, and the cell door opened. He began his transformation into a man.

"No, Shaw, keep your wolf form. There is no more time left, plus you can travel faster on four legs than on two." Arose flung the door open wide. The transformation reversed, and the wolf approached Arose and stopped.

"I'm not like your mother, Shaw, you can trust me. But you have to promise me you will stop your quarrel against me." The wolf looked at her with soulful eyes.

"Go!" she screamed. The wolf jumped and ran out the door. She quickly followed.

The ground shook violently. The moment had come for the final quake that would submerge the town. Moments later, a great noise of metal twisting and bricks colliding sent dust up into the air. The jailhouse sat in a rubble heap.

The ground beneath her feet turned to a thick liquid. She struggled to walk as each step became more difficult. She felt the earth trying to pull her down. Abandoned buildings around her slipped into the wet sandy earth. The empty cobblestone streets disappeared. Traveling back to the ship would be impossible without a sure surface for Arose to step. Too far away from the docks to call for help, she still could see the main sail of The Red Spirit in the distance.

Quicksand filled her boots, pouring in though the top, passing her knees as the ground shook. The more she struggled to move, the more difficult it became to walk.

She clung tightly to the precious opalescent gem. "Bessonth! Help me!" she cried.

In the distance, high up in the sky she heard a screech. Arose looked up. The dragon Bessonth flew toward her, a black specter trailed close behind. Bessonth screeched again when she neared Arose.

She heard Bessonth's voice in her head. "Hol' up your hands for me chil'!"

Arose raised her arms and in a swoop, she caught the dragon's claws. She hung on to Bessonth's leg and traveled over the sinking town toward the Red Spirit.

She saw the people on the dock scurrying into the waiting ships. Her heart leaped when she saw Blaze still in battle with the wild boar, Ambrielle. Blaze held a wooden crate in his hand while he and Edmund pushed at the boar keeping him away from the crowd of people boarding the ship.

Cold sea spray wet the crowd who huddled for warmth. Some children, small enough, were carefully hoisted up the gangplank, passed from hand to hand until they were safely aboard. Most waited for their turn while some adults pushed and shoved their way to safety. Now completely cut off from land, the churning water surrounded them.

A loud screech came from the hull when the ship pitched against the dock. The ship's mooring line still attached the pier to the ship, keeping it from floating away.

Some people cut off from the ship by water attempted to swim. People who ventured into deeper water screamed when they slipped under the waves. Watery maelstroms inhaled water and bodies into open chasms under the sea floor.

Arose and Bessonth reached the ship's crow's nest. Just as they were about to jump down on the sails, a lightning burst tore by them, and a horrendous clap of thunder came.

"There must be a storm close," she said to Bessonth.

"No, dat be dat damn witch. Hold on, dearie."

Arose tightened her grip on Bessonth's scaly leg. She unexpectedly flipped over and flew upward, circling back toward Morel. Arose felt a tingle throughout her body as another blast brushed by them. They quickly attacked Morel head on, her black robes sparkling with her powerful sorcery.

A flap of Bessonth's wings knocked Morel out of the sky and onto the dock below. She landed near the rampaging boar and stood up. She could not gain her footing and slipped down again. She held onto the slats of the wooden dock and lay on her belly.

Bessonth took advantage of the moment of peace to land Arose on the ship's crow's nest. Arose looked inland, The Port of San Sabastian quickly disappeared under the ocean.

She climbed down the rigging on the main mast to the quarterdeck. Lashing down crates and barrels of supplies, the crew did their best to keep the townsfolk safe. They shepherded them below deck.—George, the shopkeeper, looked at home standing at the helm shouting orders over the panicking passengers.

"The captain's first mate," Arose said. George looked at her and nodded.

"Get the captain aboard and hoist the anchor or we will be torn apart." George shouted over the din. First to the capstan, Jahn Richardson pushed the full weight of his huge gut against the winch trying pull up the massive anchor. It wouldn't budge.

"I need some help!" he called.

Josiah, Simon, and Leon ran up, each grabbing a spoke.

The chain clanged as the anchor slowly rose off the ocean floor. The crew breathed a bit easier for a moment. The ship jerked to a halt when the anchor pulled back down with the weight of the rushing water. People were thrown to the floor while more than one passenger flew over the side rail, screaming as they hit the torrid water.

"Hurry, men! Lift the anchor!" George commanded. The bow creaked loudly, the sound of wood splintering while the townsfolk screamed and prayed. They tried once again, but the anchor refused to move.

"This is not working!" Josiah cried. "Can anyone else help us?"

No one on board moved. Josiah looked around at the panicked people.

Shaw Murphy walked out of the crowd. He stood casting exasperated glances while the crowd scurried. His baldhead shone as it picked up the glinting sun. The muscles in his wide shoulders flexed and twitched. He spat on his large hands as he stepped up to the bow. He grabbed a spoke and strained. Veins in his forehead popping, his arms bulged. Grimacing, he gritted his teeth and rammed his full weight into the spindle. The other four joined him.

"Heave!" he growled. Together he, Jahn Richardson, Josiah, Leon, and Simon pushed against the capstan's spokes. One link clanged as the chain coiled around the spool. Clumps of seaweed shaken loose from the ocean floor clung to the iron as the anchor lifted.

The free-floating ship started cruising quickly. Faster and faster it moved, pulled by the current as if someone or something drew them out to sea.

The boar stopped its blind rampage and began his transformation back into Harold Ambrielle. Still fastened by thick mooring ropes, the Red Spirit dragged the dock along. Water crashed over the slip of wood carrying Blaze, Edmund, Harold Ambrielle and his sister, Morel, caught in a trap of her own making.

The current tore off planks, making the once mighty dock a small raft skimming alongside the speeding ship. Morel and Harold held onto the side of the dock as water sprayed into their faces

"Board the ship, Edmund!" Blaze ran to the mooring and pulled off the rope. He held it tightly in his already cut and bleeding hands. Edmund ran up the gangplank to the safety of the ship.

"Climb on!" Blaze called to Morel and Harold. The rope slid through his hands, slicing him even more. He winced when the salt spray entered his wounds. There were only seconds to spare while the ship drifted farther from them. Blaze held fast to the end of the rope.

"Come!" he said, holding out his hand.

Morel in her bitterness spat out to him, "I know who you are! You killed my son!"

A huge wave crashed over the pier. Blaze disappeared into the brackish water.

"Blaze!" Arose cried "NO!" Her fingers gripped the side of the ship. She hung over the guardrail gazing down into the sea.

The passengers searched the water for him.

"There he is!" George cried, pointing him out.

Blaze still clung to the mooring rope. Pulled to the surface of the water, he gulped for air and tried to hang on.

"Drop anchor!" Edmund called to the crew. The anchor slammed into the water and quickly hit bottom. The ship creaked as the anchor held onto the seabed and spun to a halt. Most of the crew lost their footing and fell to the deck. George hung onto the wheel, steadying it in the dizzying spin.

Blaze floated face down. The people on deck gazed down at him.

Arose stood on the bridge of the ship looking down at the swirling ocean. The strong undertow caught Blaze and he sunk, lifeless, beneath the water's churning surface. The rope he had clung to hung limply in the choppy sea, bobbing along with the white capped water tossing it. Arose's lungs refused air, caught instead in her throat. She felt a numbness in her fingers and felt the bobbing of the rope in her gut. George hastily slid down the rope ladder and looked over its surface but did not dare to enter its deadly waves.

Everyone on deck let out a deep gasp. Word spread rapidly and passengers strained to catch a last glimpse of the mighty captain, only to see scattered debris and nothing more. Some people wept and made the sign of the cross, holding their young ones close. Men placed their hats over their hearts and looked down sadly. They had all given him up for dead.

However, Arose knew better, Blaze could see and touch her spirit form. They had made love while she was pearlescent before him. He could reach into her and touch her soul. She had to take the chance to save him.

Chapter Eighteen
From The Depths

Arose approached the rail and reached for the mystic Gem of the Red Spirit. Edmund ran to her side. He grabbed her wrist before she touched the gem.

"Don't do it, Rosie," he whispered in her ear. "I can't bear to lose you both." The usually calm and cool Admiral had tears in his eyes.

"You do understand, Uncle, I am his only chance!"

"You are the bravest person I have ever known." He kissed the back of her hand, and she held his tightly.

She gave him a half smile. "Keep out a weathered eye," she said wryly.

She closed her eyes, pushed her spirit from her earthbound body, and looked back at herself. She had done this many times before, but this time things felt eerily different. She watched her body collapse into her uncle's arms. He lifted her up gently and carried her to the captain's quarters. Her head fell back and her arms were limp, her long hair nearly touching the floor. He rounded the corner toward the large wood double doors.

Suddenly she began to wonder how much time she had in spirit before the cord and its connection would begin to disintegrate. Questions flashed in her mind; what if the cord ripped from her while caught in the swell? If she left her soulless body for too long a spirit, any spirit wandering past could claim her body.

Her mind's eye flashed into her future. She saw herself standing on a windswept cliff overlooking the sea. Blaze stood in the distance. The pain of love, unmistakably, in his eyes when he caught sight of her. He loved her and would be here for her forever.

The vision only took seconds, but in those few moments, she saw her life with him, until the end, still in love in each other's arms. Her stomach flipped, and her heart ached. Arose decided she would do whatever she could to find him and bring him back, no matter what the cost.

While her earthbound body lay in the captain's quarters, her spirit-form dove into the ocean. The brackish waters made it difficult to see. Dirt and debris flowed through and around her. Splintered chunks of wood, rocks and ocean floor blocked her way. Tugging on her lifeline, she swam deeper and farther out to sea. Finally, she spotted him trapped in the vortex of a maelstrom, spinning at a dizzying pace. The suction of the underwater tornado dragged him into a fissure in the broken seabed.

She reached out with her gossamer hand and pulled at him. The whirling water sucked at her. Spinning in tandem with Blaze, helpless, but at least she had found him. Now she must free them both from the swirling whirlpool. Arose held him in her arms, the silver cord tangling around them.

The lifeline strained, tearing beyond repair. She had only moments to spare before the silver cord severed, leaving her soulless body on the ship. Bessonth warned her of the dangers of being a live soul in the spirit world. She had to wake Blaze or she and he would be lost forever.

She tugged at him, trying to escape the suction of the vortex, but the vacuum continued to pull them down. The hole almost under Blaze's dangling feet would tear them apart when they entered it.

Arose put her lips to his and blew her spirit-breath into his mouth. Her energy soared out of her and into Blaze. Large bubbles floated up around him. He blinked his eyes open and smiled at her translucent figure.

She looked at him, weakened from the transfer, and pointed down at the fissure in the ocean floor. He held her tightly and scanned the area. A long board swirled around them among the debris. Blaze landed his feet on it and caught the edge of the funnel. The board shot out of the cyclone, jettisoning them to the surface.

"Look, there he is!" a young boy shouted.

George and Shaw clung to the rungs of the rope ladder on the side of the ship. Blaze swam to them, and they pulled him from Arose's arms. He looked behind him and reached for her, caressing her ghostly cheek. Unseen, Arose watched while the men carried Blaze onto the ship.

A thunderbolt shot from the sky, hit the water very close to her. Arose looked up and saw Morel, standing on a black cloud. Harold looked small and shriveled next to his large looming sister.

"Yes, I see you!" Morel said. She was covered in what looked like black shining scales. The evil in her black shroud had soaked into her skin. In her clawed hand, she held a thick chain, which rose into the clouds. "You can't hide from me. Look, I have someone here to visit your cold dead body."

Morel yanked at the chain. Bessonth flew out of a high cloud, the links tight around her neck. Bessonth gasped and choked uncontrollably, once again Morel's prisoner.

"Leave her alone, witch!" growled Arose.

The last remaining strands of the cord pulled her back into her body. She awoke and took a deep breath and gasped to fill her lungs.

She recognized the room. She sat on the bed she had awoken from days before when the Blaze took the opalescent gem from her chest. The room remained silent, despite the activity going on outside the door. Candles surrounding her gave only the minimum light. She squinted into the dark. A thin layer of gauze covered her body; they had already given her up for dead.

Ripping the filmy material from her face, she sat up carefully, so dizzy from being still for so long. She held the opalescent gem in her hand, hoping for strength and warmth to come from it. Nothing.

Still weak from giving her life energy to Blaze, she tumbled to the floor. She willed her numb legs to move. She rose and stumbled to the door, urging herself on to help Bessonth.

An explosion came within feet of the doorway. The rafters shook over her head, fires started on deck and smoke billowed in.

Shouts and screams let her know Morel had them under attack.

"Get some buckets!"

"Put out the fire!"

"Women and children! Head to stern!" She looked into the blackness of the Gem of the Red Spirit. "Where are you, my little friend?" she said. "I need your help. Give me your strength!"

She heard another crash, and once again, the lightning flashed into the darkened room. The spirit peeked out at her from a dark corner of the opalescent gem.

"We can do this, my friend! You and me! You heard Uncle, we are strong, and we are brave! Are you ready?" The Red Spirit spun until the stone filled with red and orange color. Arose inhaled deeply and left the room to the main deck. Her legs were shaky, unable to carry her full weight. She used the wall to hold herself up.

Blaze looked exhausted when he caught sight of her hunched over and limping to the open deck but he jumped to attention and ran to her side. Morel angrily sent shocks through her fingers setting fires all over the ship. Blaze pushed through the crowd to her and squeezed her tightly, using his body to hide her from Morel.

"Edmund, give me Arose!" Morel demanded.

"She is not mine to give, woman. But if she were, you still would not lay a finger on her." He held the point of his longsword toward her.

A warm glow surrounded Arose and Blaze. A transfer of strength back to Arose made them glow in an ethereal essence. She stood more firmly, feeling warmth return to her legs. He placed his hand on the back of her head and stroked her hair. His beard pressed against her cheekbone as he kissed her temple. She pulled away and looked into his somber eyes.

"If you need me, I am here," he said.

"I'm sure I will, Blaze," she answered with a nod. He gave her hand a reassuring squeeze.

Arose tore herself from Blaze and pushed through the panic-stricken passengers to the rail of the ship. When people saw Arose, they backed away.

"Here I am, Morel, and you will never get the opalescent gem from me!"

"Give it to me, girl, and I will let you all live." Morel held out her claw of a hand, her long black nails, like talons, glistening with sparks.

"For what? If you open the gates of the Netherworld, the demons will devour your soul, along with the rest of us. You are not strong enough to control them. You will damn us all, and I won't let you do it!"

Leaping to stand on the rail, Arose held the amulet before her, her spirit more defiant than ever and eyed Morel.

"Shaw told me I have to die to sever the cord."

"That's never been in my plans. You will not die, Arose, oh no. You will become a dragon like Bess. This is the curse of the opalescent gem, and your family line. You will live forever, but as a dragon!" Morel's voice cackled in laughter over the storming sea.

"Morel, you deceived me. Me! Your own flesh and blood. You told me I can still have her after you took the Gem of the Red Spirit," Ambrielle shouted.

"Shut up, Harold, or you will get nothing."

"You don't understand half of what the opalescent gem can do!" Morel screeched. "Give it to me! I will sever its tie to you. And in return, I will set the beast free, and you can live in the skies."

A realization hit Arose. Like Bess when this life ended, she would be reborn into a dragon, not only because she had been the bearer of the opalescent gem, but also because Bess, the old gypsy, had been her kin from the start.

"Bess? We are family?" She smiled. Happiness and love welled up inside her.

"You are the chil' of my granddaughter. My blood is in you," Bessonth announced.

Morel shook madly, her hackles rising. She gritted her teeth and summoned her powers. She pointed her fingers at Bessonth and with a mighty blast, shocked the captive dragon. Flashes of white light danced over her from her nose to tail. The motion of her wings stopped. She dropped into the waiting ocean. Morel let go of the chain, and it followed Bessonth into the swirling tide.

Arose's heart broke into pieces and sank along with her beloved Bessonth. Disappearing, consumed by darkness in the ocean abyss. Arose looked up at Morel's black soul through the façade of beauty she held for everyone else. She saw the ugliness and jealousy, which consumed the Voodoo priestess. She saw what Bessonth had seen—a sad, envious, evil woman.

Morel pointed her sparking claw in Arose's direction. Thanks to her trip through time Arose knew what she had to do. How she could best combat the priestess. She held the Gem of the Red Spirit.

Connecting with her wild heart the Gem came to life and surrounded her in mist. A lightning shock emanated from Morel's fingertips and spread out over the ocean toward the golden sphere.

The globe not yet fully surrounding her, Blaze grabbed the cover from a sugar barrel and leapt in front of Arose who revolved inside the cloud. He shielded her from the shock with the circle of wood. The wood absorbed the lightning into its surface. It charred and turned black. He landed next to Arose with a tumble and came to his feet. Morel looked at Blaze, piercing him with her cold eyes. He challenged her stare, throwing the smoking shield into the ocean.

Morel and the crew on deck watched Arose in a mist of orange and red rise up. She silently floated above the middle deck; the only sound was the rush of the rising tide. A slow and distant rumbling began, a low steady, the rhythm rose into a noise as loud as a crash of a hundred trees felled in a forest.

The vibrations cracked the crystal shell and fire exploded outward. From the smoky remnants leapt a golden horse, Arose astride on its back holding firmly to the reins.

Her torso tightly wrapped in golden armor, white silk flew in the air behind her. Her eyes were keen and angry, and glued to the Morel's every move. In her hand, she held a golden long sword.

Blaze threw his arms into the air. "Yea, Rosie!" he yelled. "Huzzah!"

The crowd cheered behind him, watching Arose emerge from the orange wisps.

Arose kicked her heels into the sides of the horse and swung the sword over her head.

"Yah!" she cried loudly. The horse darted out over the water, running on the wind, fire springing from its hooves.

Morel's eyes grew large while Harold fell to his knees and covered his head with his hands. "Get us out of here, Morel!" he screeched.

The black cloud carrying them retreated. Arose's sword sung when it cut through the air. The tip sliced the flesh under her jaw. Blood spurted out from Morel's neck. Wincing, she slapped her claw-like hand over the wound.

Arose turned the Fire Spirit horse and readied herself to continue the onslaught. She pointed the end of the sword at Morel and Harold, fire shot out of its gleaming end. A whip of flame hit Harold, who cringed beside Morel. Flames exploded around them. Harold's hair singed and he screamed. Morel pushed him into the water to extinguish him.

"This isn't over, girl! I will come back for you." Morel spun and quickly flew toward the devastated island. Arose took chase, but stopped when she heard a tremendous roar from the ocean.

A wall of water ten times the size of the main sail bore down on them. She had to return to the ship.

Arose kicked her heels into the horse's sides and within a few strides, the horse stomped back onto the bow of the ship.

The horse trotted proudly around the deck. Children cheered and ran to it and patted its golden mane. It disappeared into a puff of golden smoke and seeped back into the opalescent gem around Arose's neck.

Reaching out to her, Blaze pulled her to him, enveloping her in his arms. He smiled and buried his face into her hair.

"You're amazing!" He laughed. "You scared me to death, but you are amazing."

Edmund came to the couple hanging onto each other tightly. "Very nice, my children, but can you do this later when we have outrun the tsunami?"

They looked up to see the wall of water coming at them. Blaze ran to the wheel, followed by Arose and Edmund. Blaze went to work as the captain of the mighty ship. She saw the grey storm grow in his eyes as the wind lashed at his hair and clothing, a look of determination on his face.

"Passengers below!" he shouted, his commanding voice thrilling Arose. "Raise the sails!"

"What is your plan, Blaze?" Edmund called behind him while Blaze headed for the stern to steer the ship.

"We are going to head directly for it," Blaze said assuredly. "Someone climb up to the main sail. Wait for my signal to let it fly. Raise the anchor!"

Upon hearing the captain's plan, the people on deck rushed to the bowels of the ship as the wall of water crept closer. The crew hastened to carry out his orders.

Shaw headed for the main rigging. Arose ran to him. "Are you going up there, Shaw?" she asked him.

"Aye! I owe you my life, I'm doing this for Liam, and he always liked you. And Blaze is a fine man."

"I'm with you," she said.

Arose watched for a moment as Blaze commanded those around him. She gulped silently, while her breath escaped her, and blushed at herself. She grabbed the mizzenmast's rope ladder over her head and climbed it to open the sail. She went up the rungs, skirt flapping in the wind as she did, almost to the crow's nest and sat ready for her orders. The ship creaked and moaned over the swelling water.

"You ready, girl?" Shaw yelled over the wind.

"Aye!" She pulled out her engraved dagger, sand still stuck in the embossment. She readied herself to cut the line to raise the sail.

The ship's bow headed for the crest of the wave. Arose hung on, looking directly into the mouth of the monstrous tsunami.

She heard Bessonth's faint voice in her head.

"Hold on chil'."

Arose looked down into the water. The shadow of the giant dragon raced toward the ship.

"Blaze!" she cried. "Bessonth is coming!"

"Ready yourselves!" Blaze shouted, not hearing her.

The ship began to climb up the side of the wave, tilting hazardously. Arose felt the pull of gravity under her feet as she hung onto the mast, horizontal to the raising water. Barrels flew off the back of the ship. Cannonballs rolled over the edge, crashing into the water below.

About to capsize, the ship hit the wave's crest.

"Hang on, mates!" Blaze yelled. "Now!"

"Aye, Captain St. James!" Shaw exclaimed. He and Arose cut the rope; the wind swelled the sail fully.

Shaw lashed himself to the main sail, while Arose hung vertically from the crow's nest. She smiled and trusted Bessonth in her heart to save them. Looking down at the shadow beneath them, she let go of the crow's nest rail. She straightened her body and hit the water with a slice, going deep, deep down into the swell.

Bessonth swam under the bow of the ship and lifted it out of the water on her back. The ship righted and the hull skimmed the monster wave's curl. Heading for the sky, Blaze and Edmund laughed as the wings of the dragon swung over their heads.

The ship, the crew, and its homeless passengers were safely nestled between the wings of the giant dragon. Arose, who had dived into the wild waters, held onto the scaly cheeks of her great-grandmother, the great dragon Bessonth, her legs wrapped around her neck.

She turned and waved to Blaze, beckoning him to join her there. Blaze held his hand over his heart and watched as Arose laid her head down on Bessonth.

Blaze ran to the bow of the ship and jumped down, stepping carefully down the dragon's spine to her long neck and sat behind Arose. He held her waist, his large hands above her hips and below her rib cage to secure her. They watched the wave speed past below them.

Crew and passengers climbed the stairs to the bow and cheered when they saw the mighty dragon flying them to safety.

"What's our heading, Captain?" Bessonth said to Blaze.

Blaze whispered in Arose's ear. "Where would you like to go, my dear?"

"Where I was happiest," she said. "Back to the Sea of Marmara."

"At this speed we will be there by dusk," he said excitedly.

"Good. I would like to see the sunset reflected in the sails."

Bessonth nodded and continued to fly with the Red Spirit on her back. She kept going until they were clear of danger. When Bessonth finally landed, Arose recognized the cliffs and spires as Marmara. Finally, where she and the Gem of the Red Spirit would be safe from Harold and Morel.

A sweet pink and blue sky greeted them when Bessonth set them gently into the crystal water. They stood on the bow while the sun turned red and orange and reflected on their skin.

Blaze placed his arm around Arose's neck, as he stood so close she inhaled the scent of cedar and iron from him. Her long blonde waves were blowing in the wind. He dug his hand deeply into the mass of loose curls. He pulled her to him, holding the sides of her face. He leaned close.

"I love you, Arose. I always have." He sighed. "But you are so strong, I thought you would not miss me."

"I'm not strong, Blaze. It's only for you and Bessonth that I have been able to do anything." She took his hand and kissed it. "There was a hole in my heart and you have filled it. I need your strength beside me."

"You have the Gem of the Red Spirit and Bessonth. How can I compare to them?" he asked with an unsteady breath.

"What of your ladies? You have a closet full of women's clothes. Whose are they?" She attempted to keep her jealousy hidden, the entire time hating herself for asking.

"They are yours, Arose." He laughed, "I had one made for you in each town I visited. Milan, France, England. The red one you wore for the wedding I had delivered to the ship just before we boarded."

"Oh? They are all lovely. I…"

"And this ship." He flung his arms wide. "The Red Spirit. I built it for you… and me."

She looked around at the opulence of the ship. Gold filigree covered the carving of a dragon in the bulkhead. Silk sails were in place of canvas on the masts. She had never dreamed, never thought for a moment, he would show his love in so many ways. How could anyone feel this way about her?

"What is all this without you, Rosie? It's nothing, nothing if you are not here with me," Blaze murmured. He passed his hand through his hair, holding it back for a moment before it once again fell over his eyes. Arose saw in him the friend she had to leave long ago and the striking Captain he had become. She'd loved him all along.

Blaze looked down into her eyes. "There has been no one else my whole life but you. From the moment I saw you so full of fire, so fearless, even as a child, I knew I could never love anyone but you."

He knelt before her and held her hand. "Please, Arose, be my wife."

She nodded slowly, her eyes never leaving his.

"Are ye sayin' yes, child?" Edmund smiled widely.

She turned to see the crew and townspeople around them.

"Yes, yes, it is." She looked back at Blaze. "Yes, Blaze, I will, I will."

"Well then!" Edmund said. "If ye are in agreement. I can marry you here and now!"

"Uncle, *un mariage sur la croix de l'épée*? We are going to step over the crossed swords?"

"Yes, my dear, and a legal one. Throw your swords on deck!" Edmund laughed while the passengers cheered. The two placed their swords down and held hands.

Edmund stood before them. Her Aunt Josephine ran to her side. Arose smiled at her.

"Shaw?" Blaze called. Shaw Murphy walked up quizzically. "I hear you saved my ship."

"Well, I dun get the winch moving there to get the anchor up." Shaw smiled, his whole head turning a bright red as he blushed.

Blaze stuck out his hand. "Well, the best man ye be. Will you stand up for me while I wed this wench?"

Shaw took Blaze's hand in his and shook it vigorously. "Watch out for this one. She knows how to hit a man where it hurts. Still, I owe her my life." He smiled at Arose.

Edmund's voice boomed into the Marmara Sea. "All here present bear witness while Blaze St. James and Arose Du Mouchelle come together to be one in spirit. Not to lose themselves in their union but as a promise of a new life. We come to share in their joy and ask the infinite powers to bless their union. We seal these two in marriage. A marriage where, at its deepest core, is love."

A silver cord appeared in the air as an orange wisp flew by. Edmund lifted the cord up and held it in his hand. He wound it around their hands as he spoke.

"Arose, do you promise to love Blaze without hesitation, to cherish and honor him?"

"Yes." She surprised herself with how easily the word came out of her mouth.

"Blaze, do you promise to love Arose without hesitation, to cherish and honor her?"

"Yes. With all my heart, Edmund," Blaze said

Edmund smiled at the two. "By the power given to me by being the highest ranking officer on this ship..." — the crowd laughed— "... I pronounce you husband and wife."

They stepped over the swords.

He looked at the crowd on deck made up of crew and villagers. "I present to you Captain Blaze and Mrs. Arose St. James."

Blaze placed his mouth on her neck and gently cascaded kisses down to her shoulder. She rose up on her toes to lean in farther. He responded by holding her tightly around her waist until she felt the air in her lungs begin to burst. She kissed him deeply, the silver cord tied to her heart wound around their hands.

She pushed him away quickly and with an imp-like grin, leapt up to the rigging. She climbed into the sails higher and higher to just below the crow's nest and lay down in its bellows, staring up into the darkening sky.

Blaze appeared before her. "The sun is about to set."

"The night is rising," she said gently.

Everything around them was bathed in pink and blue, like the sails she watched from the Jamaican cliffs.

Blaze pulled off his linen shirt. She looked closely at his chest. She saw firsthand the remnants of his life at sea and how difficult things had been for him, until now. He lay down quietly beside her and watched the stars burst over the eastern sky.

***

Weeks later, Arose stood on the brightly painted balcony overlooking the wide harbor of Marmara. The silk sheet clung to her naked body as the salty breeze caressed her skin, her loose curls blowing. She scanned the sea for the familiar sails of the Red Spirit.

A warmth surrounded her, like a velvet cloak, when her eyes settled on the flags at its highest mast. The highly polished bowsprit glistened as it caught the first morning's light. The figurehead resembling an ethereal Arose decorated the tip of the prow, staring out to the waiting sea, daring adventure to come.

She looked down as Blaze's thick forearms as they wrapped her in the dark red velvet coverlet of their bed. He nuzzled into her dense hair. She smiled as she settled her head into the crook of his arm.

"Let's go back to bed," he whispered in her ear. "Reggie will be up with breakfast soon."

"You would like that. Wouldn't you?" She giggled, his beard tickling the nape of her neck, his warm breath tingling, cascading over her.

"I have to be here right now—something is coming."

"What is?" he asked, looking out to the horizon with her.

"I'm not sure. I just know I have to be here right now."

Blaze waited a moment and gazed down at her.

"Far be it for me to doubt you." He laughed and waited a moment longer. Arose felt the heat from his body becoming more intense. She melted farther into his chest, listening to the beat of his heart becoming more rapid.

She closed her eyes. The dreams of her past had become the comforts of her present. Her visions had foretold this moment; she could now stop her search.

A rush of cool air poured over them. Their moment quickly ended when she opened her eyes. Floating before them were the amber eyes of the Dragon Bessonth.

"Hello, my children." Bessonth smiled as Arose reached up and touched her gently.

Happiness had found Arose once again. She was finally home and safe in the company of old friends and new family. Captain and Mrs. Blaze St. James were ready to pursue their new lives and the adventures that awaited them.

***

Back in the bog in the old brightly covered wagon, Morel sat at the workbench where Bess wound the gold around the Gem of the Red Spirit all those years before. Anger and revenge resonated in her mind. She concentrated deeper and deeper, until she heard a small voice in her head.

"Hello? Hello?" the voice called out.

"Where are you?" asked Morel.

"I'm floating in the water. It's dark, I can't see."

"What's your name? Who are you?"

"Madeline," came the reply.

Harold entered through the slat door. It slammed, shaking Morel from her trance. The chimes hanging from the ceiling rang out noisily.

"So what are we going to do?" he barked.

"We are going to wait," she shot back.

"For what? How long? I don't want to hang around the plantation too much, those people are a bore." He spoke in a high pitch voice to mimic the Du Mouchelles. "Where did the servants go? Who is going to cook dinner? The woman won't lift a finger and I'm not going to!"

"Enough of your complaints, Harold!" She held up her hand as he fell dumb. "We have to wait, and we will have another chance to retrieve the Gem of the Red Spirit."

"How long?" Harold whined again.

"Nine months." She glared into her mind's eye to listen again for the small voice. "Nine months, and it will all be ours."

About Andrea Roche

Andrea is a dreamer and scribbler, whose work embraces her strong matriarchal heritage. She hopes her writing will instill in her readers the idea that a woman can find their independence while keeping homegrown values.

Still living in her childhood home, Andrea hears the voices of her past. She has relied on them to tell her stories. "My mother always said I would find my way. I never knew what she meant until after she was gone. Then her voice came loud and clear, and I used it to write this book," she says.

Wife of twenty-five years and mother of three children, she had dedicated her early life to helping her family business grow. She now works for the city of New York. Five years ago, she found herself in the hospital. A simple trip home from work went awry, breaking her hip. Not used to being idle, six months in a wheelchair gave her the time to write. It was there her mind was once again allowed to wander.

Starting with her vivid imagination, she scrolled through pictures of her honeymoon in Jamaica; her mind went back into the past. Not her past, but the past of others who could have lived in a large mansion at the top of a hill covered in sugar cane. She stepped into a world with vivid colors and magic. Having already developed a polish to her writing abilities while gaining a B.A. degree with a dual major in Marketing and English Literature, she wrote what she saw and what she heard as if someone whispered in her ear.

Andrea's hard work and long hours have paid off. Upon completion of her manuscript, she described feeling the same whoosh she felt when she delivered her children into the world. She is thankful she can bring her work to her readers.

Social Media Links:

Facebook: www.Facebook/NightsArose

Twitter: www.twitter.com/Rose121562 @Rose121562

Blog: www.andrearoachauthor.blogspot.com

Acknowledgements

My gratitude goes out to so many people who read and offered their comments, allowed me to repeat verbatim every word said, sat with me for hours on end while I talked things through, for it was in those moments and most of all - through their eyes, I was able to see my story to completion. Thank you for your remarks and assistance.

My thanks go out to the Solstice Publishing and K.C. Sprayberry for your work on this book thanks for seeing what I saw. Thank you Carissa Taylor, Alicia Dean, and Gay Walley, who help and wealth of knowledge kept my story focused and polished. Thank you Bill Webb, Sandrine Moore-Straw, Donna Dimino, Patricia Staten, and Albert Munoz for your help in design, working with you is a pleasure. Thank you to my sisters and Parents for supplying me with the fodder for a story, and thanks to the folks at the Kowalinski Post 4, especially John Cinamo, who pointed out when I wrote too "froufrou." Thanks for keeping me motivated and grounded.

Cheers to my POTCO friends, who sat with me for hours while I spun my tall tales. It was there on the dock of

Padres we danced a jig and Arose sprung to life. A special thank you to: Josiah, Lizzie, Larry Dean, David, and D.K., thank you Dread Poet for letting me up on the rock in the grotto to speak some lines and get enough confidence to spur me on.

Finally, I would like to acknowledge with gratitude the love and support of my husband Michael and our children; you all were the backbone of my imagination, the lines keeping me tethered even when my mind was set to soar. Mike, thanks for waiting till 4 a.m. before calling me to bed. Elizabeth, thanks for bringing your own version of a hapless trio into the house for my entertainment. To my sons Michael and Andrew, thanks for keeping me going, and thanks to Abby for keeping my feet warm.

Just know this book would not have been possible without all of you!